6/22

To: Rich and
his wonderful
main squeeze!
I hope you enjoy

Q

Q. J. Zephyr

The 9 Orders: The Collection

This is a work of fiction. Names, characters, places, and incidents are either the product of the author's imagination or are used fictitiously. Any resemblance to actual persons, living or dead, events, or locales is entirely coincidental.

First paperback edition May 2022

Book Design by MDW Design LTD

ISBN
(978-0-578-38859-5)

ISBN
(978-0-578-38858-8)

Published by MDW LTD Publishing, LLC

www.the9orders.com

Q. J. Zephyr

Discover *The Nine Orders: The Collection* online and get involved on social media.

Scan this QR code to order more copies of this book, send some to friends and family, and discover what's next from Q. J. Zephyr!

Follow @TheNineOrdersBooks
on Instagram and Facebook to get fan exclusive merch and more!

Q. J. Zephyr

The Nine Orders: The Collection

By Q.J. Zephyr

*This book is dedicated to the loving memory of the two
finest grandfathers a boy could ever have known:
Warren C. Jones and Roger L. Swan.*

Q. J. Zephyr

TABLE OF CONTENTS

Q. J. Zephyr

Prologue

On June 21st, 2025, the skies over the earth filled with a red haze. Soon, afterward, surface temperatures on the planet rose to triple digits. The top scientific minds in the world determined that solar flares, stronger than any recorded in human history, were lashing the Earth. These flares, over the course of a few weeks, would intensify until they reached cataclysmic proportions. The good news was that the storms would subside after a few months. The bad news was that they would incite earthquakes, tsunamis, and volcanic eruptions not to mention the fallout from increased exposure to solar radiation. All of these factors would spell an end to most mammalian species on the planet unless measures were taken to protect them. Panicked citizens of every nation demanded to know what, if anything, their governments were going to do to save them.

The leaders of the free world convened in Geneva to find a solution for the oncoming crisis. While no one country possessed the technology to mitigate the effect of the solar flares, they did have the means to evacuate a good portion of their populations from the surface of the earth. Most developed countries had secretly built fallout shelters called DUMBs (deep underground military bases) during the onset of the cold war. These DUMBs had originally been constructed to house the heads of state in the event of a nuclear attack. The new plan called for these same structures to be used as temporary shelters accessible to all lawful citizens within their nation's borders. Unfortunately, after everything was said and done, the combined capacities of the DUMBs would only be able to house a third of the global population. And while the United States, China, and France's DUMBs were large enough to accommodate their populations and more, other countries' facilities could not. This meant that every method of safely housing people from the storms had to be used. After tapping every abandoned subway system and missile silo on the planet, engineers were confident that they could greatly increase the total number of people they could save. There was nothing that could be done for the rest of the world: undocumented immigrants, felons, and many of society's malcontents. Those left out of the shelters would have to fend for themselves while the surface of the earth was ravaged.

As the underground shelters were being stockpiled with food, water, and medicine UN leaders quickly took stock of the logistical challenges they faced. Global martial law was instituted. NATO forces, swelling with the soldiers from every corner of the world, were put in charge of enforcing the global mandate. Citizens were given 45 days to report to their nearest civic venue (airport, train station, stadium, etc...) to register for the shelters in a process that came to be known as the 'collection'. Frustration rapidly grew over the collection centers' waiting periods, their institutionalized prioritization, and their refusal to accept pets of any kind. Passionate protesting and violent rioting broke out all over the world. In response, NATO shock troops meted out punishment with vicious efficacy. Without hesitation, zealous soldiers killed dissidents of any nationality who didn't respect curfews, collection center employees, or other emergency ordinances.

The pressure put on families to protect themselves rapidly increased with the passing of every day. The freeways became clogged with people trying to make it to cities whose populations were smaller searching for quicker, safer lines at the collection centers. And with the government's 45-day deadline looming, a final surge of people made desperate journeys in hopes that they would find shelter from the oncoming storm.

The 9 Orders: The Collection

Q. J. Zephyr

Chapter 1: On the Road

Nick slammed the tailgate of his pickup shut forcing the dulled latch to catch. He gave the taut tie downs that crisscrossed the truck's bed one last tug. Everything he needed to sustain life on the road had been packed up. He walked to the cab of his '79 Ford and pulled open the driver's side door. The hinge squealed under the weight of its steel frame. He fished out a full bottle of 151 from underneath the driver's seat. Twisting the cap off, Nick took a good, long swig. A cool rush washed over him as the slippery liquid coated his lips, his tongue. It had been four years since his last sip of alcohol. He savored the taste by pressing his lips against the fronts of his teeth. Nick pulled out a dirty rag from his back pocket, stuffed it into the bottle's open mouth, then lit it with his Zippo. He hurled the Molotov cocktail through the living room window of the house he had bought for his ex-wife and had been living in for the last 7 years, without her.

The sound of shattering glass beckoned Nick to draw closer to the growing blaze. His eyes glassed over, not from emotion but from the short distance which he now stood from the fire. He had left so many things inside the house and as their edges peeled and their veneers bubbled Nick felt freed from a life that had never quite been his own. Nick walked away from the inferno filled with the conviction that he had made the right decision not to register for the collection. He climbed into his truck and paused, staring for a moment into his rearview. Bright orange tongues of flame licked the crumbling interior of the once-proud home. Arnold, Nick's bulldog who shared the front seat, eyed his master woefully. He couldn't understand Nick's decision to torch their home, the only home the dog had ever known. Nick gave Arnold a reassuring pat on the head before starting the engine and pulling out of the driveway. He drove his cream-colored pickup through a maze of abandoned single-family homes until he came to the onramp that led to the interstate. He turned onto it and headed northeast toward the San Gabriel Mountains.

Nick's army pal, Tommy, had a hunting lodge outside of Lake Arrowhead. Tommy had offered to put Nick up for the duration of electromagnetic storms. In return, Nick had agreed to go hunting with him, stocking Tommy's freezers before the weather got really bad. It was an excellent setup. Nick could use the company which he hoped would serve as a distraction from the demons that had been plaguing him his entire life.

The reddened sky stretched over the interstate like a slab of meat stretched between two stakes. Nick felt as though he were coursing through the stiff, ashened arteries of an exhumed colossus. As he drove across the empty lanes of a desolate freeway he became increasingly aware of all the tread marks left behind by decades of skidding tires. It was something he had never paid attention to before. Their fading imprints reminded him of the first and only car accident he had ever been in. He and his ex-wife were on their first official date. They were headed to the wedding of a mutual friend when Victoria's sedan got sideswiped by a large SUV. The driver was lit two sheets to the wind. The car folded in on them piercing their soft flesh and snapping their strong bones. Nick and Victoria, caged in steaming metal and fiberglass, lay so close together they could've kissed had their mouths been aligned. As their blood pooled together here and there, Nick's calm voice talked them through the pain and the uncertainty of that moment. After the Jaws of Life pried them free, Nick's connection with Victoria remained. Somewhere within the brutality of that moment, they had fallen in love. They were married less than a year later.

Nick had made plenty of trips to Tommy's cabin- a true man's retreat filled with beer, bourbon, bullets, and beef jerky. He knew the way but preferred driving it at night. Route 11 was chock full of steep, deadly switchbacks that allowed very little room for user error. The shifting cloak of night muffled the abysmal drop-offs and made the drive much more palatable. During the twenty mile climb, two motorcycles joined Nick on the lonely mountain road. The ex-soldier had thought he was being followed by a single car before seeing the headlights split apart in his mirror. They were a couple of Hell's Angels out looking for trouble. The bikers peered greedily into the cab of Nick's truck before gunning their engines and screeching off into the night. Nick counted his lucky stars they hadn't tried anything. There was no telling how employing evasive maneuvers on a lonely mountain pass would shake out.

Nick finally made it to the top of the grade and pulled over to let Arnold out for a much-needed potty break. He had to go too and stepped to the edge of a cliff to relieve himself. He took in the view of the flatlands below. The vast emptiness before him was blanketed by a pure, dense blackness. The few lights that could be seen appeared as though they were distant stars in the night sky. Nick sensed danger emanating from their glow. It was as if they were trying to lure him into the mouth of a hidden predator. Who were those brave souls down there broadcasting their presence for anyone to see, Nick wondered? After zipping up his fly he called out to Arnold and the two of them hopped back into the pickup and kept on.

Nick found the turnoff to Tommy's without incident. It was an unpaved fire road that had recently been rebuilt after flooding out the year before. Surrounded by dense pine groves on either side the road was barely wide enough for two cars to pass. The old Ford handled the bumpy terrain just as well as the first day Nick's father had driven it home from the dealership. The truck had been Nick's high school graduation present and it meant the world to him. It turned out to be the last thing his father had given him before suffering from a fatal stroke just months after Nick's high school graduation. His old man had been a tragic figure, a victim of the bottle, and the apple didn't fall far from the tree.

Coming close to the end of the fire road, Nick made out the familiar silhouette of Tommy's cabin in the distance. Its warmth seemed all the brighter against a darkening sky. The jagged tree line that stood out starkly behind the cabin reminded Nick of all the good times he'd experienced there. His shoulders rounded and he decided to take the last stretch of the road easy. He pulled his steel-toed boot off the accelerator a bit and pretended to take on the shallow bumps in the road as a skier would moguls. Arnold jumped up on all fours and glared at his master. The huge bulldog liked to reserve his strength for emergencies. He didn't like having to exert himself for something as trivial as a ride in the front seat.

Nick tried radioing Tommy from the truck but got nothing but static. As he fussed with his CB a blurred object from the right side of the road slammed into his hood before rolling off to the side. The sound of crinkling metal startled Arnold who let off one solid penetrating bark, his eyes never leaving the front of the truck. He sniffed the air and began to growl from the back of his throat. The blur appeared to be a man, but it was too dark to tell, and Nick's headlights weren't making things any easier. Whatever it was still lay by the front left tire.

Nick reached into the glove box and quickly pulled out his trusted HK. He chambered a round and slipped the safety off in one deft motion, but before he could open the door, a ragged, bearded man rose to the driver's side window. The old man looked like he had been living in a cave for years. Soot and grime covered his face, his teeth yellow and pocked. Nick's instincts told him to shoot through the glass and kill the son of a bitch right where he stood. Instead, he cracked the window an inch while aiming the muzzle of his handgun downward into the man's face.

"They're coming, y'all! No one's safe 'round here, partner. Nobody. Soon, they'll be everywhere. Heehee. If I were you, I'd turn right 'round and go back down the grade." the man's breath reeked and was bad enough to make even Arnold sneeze.

"Who's coming?" Nick asked gun at the ready. "Who's coming? Answer me!"

"Oh, that's right, that's right. You don't know, do ya? No, you don't. Haha. Trust me, partner, you don't want to. Better you get the hell outta Dodge while you still can." The old man's words croaked out of his throat as he tilted his head to speak into the crack of the window. Arnold started to bark again but this time there was a threatening snarl attached to it. It was a tone that signaled the bulldog's readiness to attack. That was Nick's cue. He sped out of there leaving the old man choking on dust. Out of the thinness of the air, they both heard gunshots ringing off into the night. By the time Nick pulled onto the gravel driveway in front of Tommy's cabin he was in no mood for shits and giggles. Tommy had heard the truck and came out to greet his best friend with open arms, but Nick wasn't having any of it. He was rattled and ready and Arnold was on full guard mode. The stout bully jumped out of the truck's cab and started lifting his leg all around the property.

"What the hell is going on around here, Tommy?" Nick asked pacing back and forth on Tommy's porch. The hollow sound of his booted steps reverberated underneath the old wooden planks that supported them.

"What are you talking about Nick?" Tommy put his arm around his friend. "What's the matter, man?"

"Some crazy asshole, I don't know, he looked like he'd been living in a damn cave his whole life. The guy jumps onto my truck while I'm driving. I must've been going 15-20mph when he slammed onto my hood."

"Haha. Yeah, that's just Dale. Everybody around here knows him. He's a little off his rocker." Tommy assured Nick taking a bit of the edge off.

"I heard gunshots back there. You're telling me that guy's armed?"

"Well, why the hell not? Everyone else around here is."

"You can't tell me that you feel safe having somebody like that wandering your property with a loaded weapon." Nick put his hands on his hips waiting for Tommy's response.

"Ugh, Take 'er easy, bud. Don't let anarchy get under your skin. So, you gotta share the world with a few crazy people, so what. I just like the fact that I don't have to pay taxes for as long as these storms last. Haha."

"He said something about it not being 'safe' around here, something or someone was coming. What was he talking about?" Nick continued trying his best to calm down.

"Enough of all that. You're here now. You're safe,
I promise. Besides, I know Jasper's dying to play
with Arnold. C'mon." Tommy went inside with Nick
and let his gigantic overly excited Rhodesian
Ridgeback out of its crate. Jasper, almost as large as
Nick in mass, bounded out of the cage licking
anything with a pulse. Arnold and Jasper were old
pals and began smelling each other end to end the
way dogs do. After they had become reacquainted
with one another they ran out back and started to
wrestle each other.

"You still on the wagon?" Tommy asked.

"I think so. Let's see if I can make it through the
week without slipping. I don't really care anymore,
to be honest with you. I've proved to myself that I
don't need to drink. And seeing as we might very
well be dead soon I don't see the point in staying
dry."

"That's the spirit. No use in me drinking alone,
not when there's the company to keep. But I'm not
gonna offer you anything. There are sodas in the

fridge if you want one but I'm drinking straight whiskey startin' right now!" Tommy led Nick through the cedar cabin and into the outdated linoleum-floored kitchen. Tommy poured himself three fingers worth of J&B, plopped a big ice cube in his glass, and gestured for Nick to help himself. Nick got a Sprite and the two went out back to the enormous fenced-in backyard where Jasper was busy showing Arnold the digs. Tommy headed to his smoker and lifted its barrel-shaped lid to check on dinner. Nick's nose filled with the beautiful aroma of barbecued meat. He looked inside the smoker and beheld an expertly prepared rump roast dripping fat on the red hot hickory chips below. Nick's mouth watered. He was no chef and had been living off cereal, poorly cooked steak, and take-out for as long as he could remember.

"You like it now, huh? Wait 'til you taste it. I pumped a garlic celery puree inside that sucker. Every bite's gonna be as good as the first. I guarantee it." Tommy said taking great pride in his cooking. He wasn't much for the sides but his entrees were always right on the money, restaurant quality, if not better.

"Man, I haven't smelled anything that good in a long time," Nick said as a sudden streak of lightning crashed down a mile away ripping through the trunk of a pine tree. Its smoldering remains fizzled and creaked before falling to the ground. The flash of electricity was followed by a peal of thunder that seemed as though it would break the sky in two. Arnold and Jasper immediately stopped what they were doing, ears perked, and waited for what would come next rain. The downpour was instant and heavy. Nick helped Tommy bring the food inside after locking the smoker shut. The dogs followed closely behind shaking off the water in their coats before going into the living room where dry, warm doggie beds awaited them.

"This is how it's going to be, huh?" Nick asked hanging his wet flak jacket onto a hand-turned coat rack that stood by the kitchen door.

"Pray that this is all it'll be. You heard the nerds. Three months of the most extreme weather anyone's ever seen. Something tells me that you're underestimating Mother Nature."

"I'm not underestimating anything. I just have no frame of reference. I grew up in California, remember?"

"Yeah, well I'm from Sioux Falls and it gets colder than a witch's titty up there. People die every winter from their furnaces blowing out or getting trapped in snowdrifts. It's serious business."

"Hmmm. I wonder how bad it'll get?"

"One way or the other, we're gonna find out," Tommy replied plating slices of the roast. "We gotta get out there and hunt for our food now before it's too late. It's been more than a few months since I went out there lookin'. To be honest, I don't exactly know where the game's gone too."

"Where else would they be if not up here in the mountains?" Nick asked sarcastically.

"I don't know. Animals can sense bad weather. They follow their instincts. For all, we know the deer are on their way to Death Valley."

Tommy always made Nick think. It was one of the reasons why they were still friends. Nick was a bit obtuse about a lot of things in life, but he made up for it with toughness and decisive action. Tommy was the one who could think things through. But on more than one occasion Tommy had come to a similar endpoint as Nick who had simply followed his gut. Tommy respected him for that and was truthfully a little jealous of Nick's cavalier ability to handle complex situations and still come out on top.

"You know, Tommy, you never really told me why you didn't register for the collection. Why'd you choose to stay up here anyway?"

"Contingencies," Tommy answered without hesitation.

"Contingencies?"

"The option that readily avails itself to the observer ain't always the soundest one. All those people crowding in underground bacteria incubators smacks of desperation and a severe lack of foresight." Tommy brought the plates of food to the kitchen island that was ringed on one side with bar stools. The two of them sat down and began chowing down on roast, baked potatoes, and canned pork beans. "A lot of people are going to get sick. Mark my words. Too many germs, man. You thought boot camp was bad. I doubt they'll even have enough food for everybody. And what if these storms last longer than anyone expects? They'll be forced to start kicking people out into the open. There's just too many things that could go wrong down there. I'd rather take my chances on the surface. I can last a year up here or more if I have to, weather permitting."

"But what about all the risks? You and I might just be sitting ducks up here."

"Sitting ducks can fly. Sardines in a can can't go anywhere. Now that cellar downstairs is insulated, warm in the winter, cool in the summer, and jam-packed with tons of cool shit I've collected over the years. I got a composting toilet down there, some astronaut ice cream...hell, I've even got a water purification system ready to go. Hell, I'm catchin' all the rainwater right now in a 600 gallon tank out back. Yeah, I'd place my bets on us any day."

"Well, I'd rather eat like this than the C-rations they're probably feeding everybody underground."

"I doubt they're even eating C-rations, man. They're probably feeding 'em cornmeal like livestock to decrease the need for going number two. You remember those high-carb diets A-School? We'd go weeks without taking a dump."

"Yeah, I remember. I hadn't thought of that. That's a lot of sewage."

"Sure is. Where they gonna put it all? Now I've got a freshly drained septic tank that will last me until I'm an old man. I'm not saying I can survive out here indefinitely, but a few months should be a piece of cake as far as supplies go."

"This is roast is friggin' awesome," Nick said with a full mouth. He scarfed his food down a little too quickly. Tommy realized that Nick probably hadn't eaten properly in a long time.

"We aim to please. Hey, I've got a damn good movie picked out for tonight."

"Oh yeah, which one?"

"Jurassic Park! The first one."

"Oh yeah? I love the first one. The rest are crap, but the first one's badass."

After dinner, Nick and Tommy went into the living where the dogs were already snoozing and plopped down on a large comfy chamomile sofa. Tommy had made buttered popcorn from scratch straight off the skillet. The smell of the warm, salty butter lifted the dogs from their naps. The two friends threw a couple of kernels to their four-legged pals then settled in for a relatively quiet evening. They would hunt tomorrow. Their lives could very well depend on what they could first find and then kill. The guys had drifted off and slept through a moment where Jasper and Arnold both were on the alert. Had the guys been more focused on their immediate surroundings they might have sensed the strange figure observing them from outside the living room window. The dark silhouette, hidden behind the tall trunks of shedding pine trees, heard Arnold's low, guttural growl and went slinking off back into the wet forest.

Chapter 2: Eight Points

Nick got up early the next morning and went outside to greet the new day. Arnold shook off his sleep and dutifully followed. They both relieved themselves by a stand of pine trees south of the cabin. Nick looked up at the pale blue sky. The rising sun's corona lit the underbelly of the few stratus clouds that drifted lazily about. If it wasn't for the impending doom of the storms Nick would have considered himself to be in paradise. The pair were about to walk back inside when something caught Arnold's attention. He was sniffing the ground outside the living room window and making a fuss about whatever he'd found. Nick walked over to inspect and was surprised by what he saw. Just below the window, there was a pair of large, oddly shaped footprints a half-inch deep. For the life of him, Nick couldn't identify the animal that had made them. Whatever made those prints was heavy and bipedal. Nick tried to track the prints south deeper into the woods but lost the trail among the freshly fallen pine needles that covered the forest floor. Maybe the same crazy old man that jumped onto the hood of his truck had made them as part of a practical joke or something. Nick decided he would ask Tommy about them once he was awake.

Nick went back inside and fed Arnold. He then cracked open some eggs and began making breakfast for two. The slow, meandering scent of frying bacon woke Tommy who'd been sleeping in the next room. Tommy slowly stretched his body before groggily slinking into the kitchen. He slumped down onto one of the stools and laid his arms and head down on the tapioca-colored island.

"Smells pretty damn good," Tommy muttered as he shielded his eyes from the morning light. He looked like he had just been electrocuted. Broad shafts of jet black hair stood straight up from the top of Tommy's head.

"I should dress you in a plaid flannel and put you in a cornfield."

"Haha," Tommy plopped down onto a barstool. "Pigs and chicken, huh? You know how to cook?"

A flash of nostalgia for his married life flashed through Nick. "I don't cook unless it's for someone else. I just don't bother when I'm by myself. Sounds pretty sad, but it's the truth."

"Ah, gotcha. Well, let's see if you're any good." Tommy said lifting his head off the island.

Nick slid Tommy's breakfast in front of him along with a tiny bottle of Tabasco.

"Hey, when I was outside taking a whizz earlier I found a pair of really strange tracks in the mud underneath that window over there. They're fresh. Someone or something was spying on us last night while we were watching that movie."

"It was probably just Dale again. Don't worry, he's harmless." Tommy added as he forked omelet into his mouth. "These are good."

"I don't think it was Dale. I mean, unless he's got a size fifteen foot with pointed toes. I tried to follow them, but they disappeared under the overgrowth."

Tommy waved off Nick's peculiar description. "Yeah, well, tracking is hard, man. Not everybody has the knack for it."

"What are you trying to say?"

"I'm saying my old man could've tracked 'em in a blizzard."

"Easier said than done."

"That's why not everybody can do it."

"You're kind of a dick in the morning. You know that, right?"

"No, really, my dad had a trick for everything. In the case of pine needles, he used to say that they didn't fall like regular leaves. They're heavier on one end. Regardless of which end hits the ground first, they form a pattern like a braid. But the more time goes by the harder it is to see."

"Bullshit!"

"Why don't you go outside and see for yourself, smartass?"

"You know what? I will. I'll be back." Nick made for the door eager to prove Tommy wrong. He closed it quickly behind him so Arnold wouldn't follow. Nick walked over to where the tracks were and followed them just as he had done before. Sure enough, the pine needles crossed over each other like a braid. Nick was able to track the trail carefully until it met back up with the fire road. The tracks took on a whole new dimension in the packed dirt of the road. They were huge and unlike anything Nick had ever seen before. There was no way for him to know for certain, but the prints looked like they had been made by a large bipedal animal with claws. Its tracks disappeared over a slope washed out by the rain on the opposite side of the road.

Nick ate a slice of humble pie before returning to face Tommy. When he opened the door to the kitchen nobody was there, not even the dogs. Nick grabbed a soda from the fridge and listened out for them. He heard sounds coming from out front and went outside. Tommy was busy stuffing packs with everything they would need for a profitable hunt.

"You were right," Nick admitted.

"Yeah, my old man was freaky like that. He took hunting pretty seriously. I don't think he bought meat from a grocer, ever. Well, maybe for Christmas and shit, but that's it."

"You should come and take a look at those tracks before they disappear. I've never seen anything like 'em."

"Alright, alright. I'll give 'em a gander on our way out." Tommy agreed without looking up. Sweat was dripping from his head as he forced a roll of toilet paper into a side pocket of one of the rucksacks.

Nick wandered around the garage gazing at all the old photos pinned to the tack board-lined walls.

He enjoyed looking at all the captured moments that seemed to belong to another world, one far removed from the present. There were even a few of him and Tommy fishing that were more than a decade old. Nick's favorite photo was of Tommy's dad as a young soldier. He was holding a flame thrower and smiling for the camera, the mean Vietnamese bush fading to white in the background. That photograph always reminded Nick of the men and women he'd served with overseas who never made it home. Their faces and voices were distant memories now, but they would always resurface now and again. Most of the important people in Nick's life had been reduced to memories or photos. Nick thought, once again, of Victoria's beautiful face. She had deserved a better life. He failed at providing it for her.

"Nick!" Tommy's voice broke through Nick's train of thought.

"Yeah, sorry, what's up?"

"Hand me those headlamps behind you. There should be a couple of battery packs over there, too."

"Yeah, no prob." Nick handed them over to Tommy who had pretty much finished packing.

"Haha, you know what time it is. Go choose your cartridge, brotha. After we break 'em apart and clean 'em up a little, we're gone." Tommy used his head to gesture toward the stairs that led down to the meat locker where his arsenal was kept. Nick beamed and clambered down the narrow stairwell. The cellar was huge and mirrored the floor plan of the cabin above. The floors and walls were covered in shotcrete which gave the interior a texturized matte finish. Nick had always thought the spartan space looked like a cold war interrogation room.

The cellar was chockful of cool stuff. Dug deep into the earthen floor sat two large vaults used to store food. On the farthest wall from the stairs stood two large metal cabinets that housed a variety of automatic and semi-automatic weapons.

Nick felt like a kid in a candy store, but he already knew which rifle he would use, the trusted 260 Remington. Nick had wonderful luck with the Remington. He had even dubbed it "R-Twelve" after downing a giant stag with the same amount of horn tips back in 2016. He'd even etched twelve small bevels in the forward land of the rifle to signify his proficiency with the weapon. Nick placed the disassembled rifle parts in a gun bucket along with two boxes of ammunition and ran back upstairs. Tommy was already cleaning the rifling of his barrel and welcomed Nick to sit down and do the same. He gave Nick a look that questioned his friend's unwavering devotion to the same weapon.

"Whaddya got there?" Nick asked checking out the carbon finish on a cartridge he was unfamiliar with.

"This, my friend, is something new out of Switzerland. It's the CZ-7. And it's rated at 4000fps at 500 yards." Tommy bragged grinning from ear to ear.

"What? Bullshit! Haha."

"Remember what happened last time you called 'bullshit'?"

"No 7mm rifle in history can boast those numbers with any kind of accuracy. You know what? Belay my last. I'm not gonna say a thing. You can show and prove. And while you're skinning your barrel, I'll be skinning my kill." Nick said satisfied with his tried and true methods. He oiled his rifle across a large worktable covered in green felt. At first glance, Tommy's garage was organized in a very bizarre fashion. To a serious gunman, however, it was heaven. Tommy had three different presses to pack shot and there were tuning instruments of all kinds scattered about. Posters of ballistic stats and used targets with handwritten notations were tacked up on just about every space available.

When both men had finished cleaning and assembling their rifles Nick put their gear in the back of Tommy's lifted Bronco. They planned on being gone for a few days and had to leave enough food out for the dogs. Arnold and Jasper would have free run of the house and could use the doggie door to access the backyard whenever they wanted. The guys said their farewells to their canine buds then jumped into Tommy's truck.

"Wait, take a look at those prints before you drive over them."

"You and these damn prints! Man, you must really miss hunting. Too much city life." Tommy said sarcastically. Nick gave him a mock look of death and Tommy immediately relented. "Okay, okay, okay. Where are they?"

"Just ahead, seventy-five yards," Nick answered quietly while the Bronco rolled closer and closer. "Okay, stop." Nick opened the door of the SUV and hopped out before it had come to a complete stop.

Tommy set the parking brake and followed. He knelt beside Nick who was already bent over examining the most extant sample of the print.

There was a moment of silence that persisted for some time as Tommy absorbed the details of what he was looking at.

"I am the Lizard King. I can do anything." Tommy muttered. He followed it up by humming a tune Nick couldn't place.

"Huh?"

"Jim Morrison, man." Tommy stood up. "Haven't you ever listened to The Doors?"

"Of course! What does that have to do with anything?"

"These are lizard tracks, Nick. C'mon. Let's get going while the sun is still climbing." Tommy huffed.

"What kind of lizard makes bipedal tracks? And of that size?"

"It's probably just some wandering Komodo dragon or somethin'. People keep weird pets up here, man. I can't say for sure if the marks are four-legged or not. Lizards make a different kind of four-legged track than mammals do. The spacing is more even with lizards. I don't see a tail drag, which is strange, but the only thing I care about is that the prints are heading away from my property."

"Okay." Nick threw up his hands. "It's all good then, I guess. Let's go." Nick lied. Everything inside him was telling him that something was wrong. But Tommy was too smart to be convinced of anything. They got back into the Bronco and headed down the fire road before turning north toward Lake Halmeth.

Tommy blasted his favorite classic rock mix as he tore down the two-lane highway without the slightest remembrance of the laws that had once governed the land. They drove for twenty minutes before Tommy pulled off the highway and turned onto a horse trail that meandered eastward into the woods. He followed the trail until it washed out onto a wide embankment at the foot of a wide creek bed. He parked the Bronco on its banks and declared the spot their base camp.

Nick was taken aback by the beauty of the entire scene which was covered in yellow and green California Maple leaves. He, too, thought it was an ideal place to begin their hunt. The creek would provide a clean water source for cooking, cleaning their kill, and filling their canteens. They both got out of the Bronco and breathed in the crisp mountain air. No mosquitos, no people, no noise-a perfect getaway, Nick thought. The weather was holding up nicely and the skies showed no signs of imminent danger. Hopefully, they could snag a couple of deer before things got bad, at least that was the plan.

"We've got plenty of daylight. I say we get a move on heading east." Tommy figured. He waited for Nick's agreement but instead found his buddy transfixed, stiff as a board. "What's up?"

"I'm feeling north. Call it intuition." Nick smiled standing like a stone in the middle of the meager creek flow. Gentle folds of water rippled over the toes of his tan work boots.

"Well, that settles it, then. Northeast it is." Tommy acquiesced.

"How about north-northeast?" Nick laughed. Tommy cracked up and the two men donned their packs and headed back over to the truck to lock it up. They placed a camo cover over it then shadowed the creek's path until it came to the foot of a hill of granite boulders. Tommy swiftly climbed to the top and surveyed the land around them while Nick remained below. Tommy stayed up there for five minutes drawing in his notepad, something he always did on his hunts. His little maps and sketches of the terrain had always proved to be pretty helpful. He eventually came back down just as quickly as he had climbed up.

"There's lots of rattlers out, Nick. Watch yer step."

"No doubt. What'd ya see up there?"

"It's game territory alright. Northeast doesn't seem bad at all. But I think we should stay on the east side of this ridgeline which goes on for quite a ways before dropping off into a bunch of canyons. That'll be our day making it over there. We'll set up camp as soon as we can see beyond the ridge."

"Cool. So do we climb up right here or what?"

"It plateaus about a half-mile to your left. We'll cut angle upward and take it easy as she goes. Should only take us fifteen, twenty minutes." Tommy said putting his notebook in the breast pocket of his hunting vest."

"Alright, let's move!" Nick began moving apace. A hunt during mid-August meant the animals would be spread farther apart from each other than if they were in mid-rut. Despite the humidity, the ground cover was dry and hot which meant the game would most likely not stray too far from water. The dryness of the forest bed meant that it was also going to make it difficult to stalk prey due to the noise of crackling foliage. Whatever they would find on the hunt would be a result of patience and long distance shooting.

The guys finally reached the lull on the hill and crossed over its shallow crest to the leeward side. Nick stopped to take a swig of cold creek water before moving on. He reveled in its taste. He could feel the coolness trace a path down his esophagus and into the tissues of his stomach. There was a lot more sun on the east side of the ridge but also more wind and cold. They descended into an expansive meadow littered with tall, wild grasses and lonely boulders while keeping a lookout for rattlesnakes. They walked in silence each man letting their imagination travel backward in time. Nick thought of the brave settlers who had once passed through the same country on horse and buggy more than a century before. The land looked Biblical, epic, and vast. By the time they reached the break in the ridgeline, the sun was setting behind Pike's Peak, the largest of the San Gabriel

Mountains. The sun spit streaks of crimson and peach across the heavens. The drama playing out in the sky reminded Nick of Ragnarok, the end of time when the gods of Asguard would be slaughtered by an army of vengeful giants. He loved Norse mythology. He wasn't an expert on it but always took the time to read anything about the Nordic culture that he came across.

They stopped and set up camp on the lip of a promontory covered in sand and seashells. Tommy built a fire ring out of loose stone while Nick searched for kindling. As soon as their fire got hot enough Nick began making squaw bread, a hunting tradition the two had shared time and time again. Tommy heated up some black beans and leftover meat from yesterday's roast. They ate quietly while marveling at the subtly changing colors of the sky. Both men felt like children again living in a world filled with wonder and adventure.

"So, you just dropped everything and drove up here, huh?" Tommy asked while cleaning his tin dinner tray with a damp rag.

"Not quite like that," Nick's eyes were transfixed on the dancing flames of the campfire.

"What else could it be like?"

"Well, I burned Vicki's house down," Nick confessed meeting Tommy's gaze, the fire between them. "I sent it to her. Maybe she can get some use out of it in the afterlife."

"Damn, bro, you burned down your house? Somebody call Dr. Phil!"

"Yeah, Arnold wasn't too happy about it. I couldn't live there through all of this and I damn sure didn't want anybody squatting in it. So, I just gave it back to Vicki. It was always hers. You know that."

"That woman was an angel, Nick. How you screwed that up I'll never understand."

"Yeah, I'll never live it down, trust me. I think about her every day, sometimes every minute."

"Well, there's nothing like a good ole hunting trip to wash away the sins of the world. Besides, man, there was no way anyone could've known she'd die like that. I mean, if she were alive today and still married to that jackass, what was his name? Walter? Anyway, if she were still married to that guy you wouldn't feel so guilty."

"Hmm. Maybe you're right," Nick sighed heavily, "I think I need a drink."

"Now, you're talking something I can understand. And you know I brought Mr. Beam and his amigo Señor Cuervo with me." Tommy didn't waste any time and poured two shots of Tequila into a couple of Dixie cups. They guzzled down the alcohol as quickly as they could turning the mundane into a competition. Tommy slammed his paper cup against his knee a few seconds before his friend who was clearly out of practice. Nick let out a gasp of air as the Tequila filled his body with calming warmth. They had forgotten about the deadly storms. For a little while, they were just two guys camping out. They talked all night about politics and the government's apparent inability to do anything right. They reminisced about their time in the Army and how it had affected them. Tommy regretfully regaled Nick with the details of his last sordid love affair with an El Salvadoran woman who had almost killed him when she caught him cheating on her with another woman. And then Tommy lit a joint and the real conversation began.

"I wonder what's going on down there. Aren't you the least bit curious?"

"Haha, those people are screwed, man. Like with big, long lag screws. The weather's not even bad up here. The government probably lied about the whole damn thing."

"Please. That's impossible. You just think everything is some grand conspiracy theory."

"Look, man, they already took everybody's money. All the money in the world is gone, brother. Poof." Tommy exploded his fingers near his lips to strengthen his point.

"How could you possibly know that?" Nick argued. He sat back with his arms folded waiting to hear Tommy's answer.

"Because the stock market has been officially shut down, Nick. Nonoperational. You don't know about money, do you? Don't worry, it's one of the reasons I like you, man. But you don't know anything about money. As soon as they stopped trading everything collapsed. Do you know what happens when a heart stops beating? And I'm not talking like for a few seconds, but a few months. You can't resuscitate it. Don't you see? There's no value in money anymore. They robbed the entire planet at one time. Why else would they want everyone to bring their tax returns with them to the collection centers?

"Let me get this straight. You're saying that when everybody comes back to the surface their bank accounts will be empty?"

"I'm saying that the monetary system, as we know it, is done for. No more sterling, no more US dollar-nothing. Gone with the wind." Tommy let out a big yawn and stretched out his long, wiry arms. The sandman must have flipped a switch somewhere in Tommy's brain. After making his point he walked over to his sleeping bag and slid inside it. Before even saying good night, Tommy was out like a light.

Nick watched his friend sleep. Tommy was unlike anyone he had ever met. Nick first met him after being recruited into C-COM (Close Combat Operations Management). Tommy had a reputation for being one of the best engineers on the base at the time. He was an expert in fabricating and dismantling explosives and incendiary devices. Their unit specialized in 'asset recovery'. If a soldier, diplomat, or civilian's safety had been compromised it was Nick and Tommy's job to retrieve them by any means necessary to save civilian casualties, at least on paper.

When Nick ended his military career and moved to the west coast Tommy followed a few years later. But the engineer refused the comforts of coastal San Diego and chose to live in the Cleveland National Forest. Tommy joked that he was close enough for Nick to make routine visits but far enough to avoid yuppies and hipsters. The two friends had been through a lot together and there was no one else in the world that either of them trusted more.

Tommy's theory about the effects of the collection on the monetary system was compelling. Nick had been naïve in thinking that when the storms subsided, he'd be able to recoup most of the losses from the destruction of his property. He now realized how rash his actions had been. Victoria had let Nick keep the house after their divorce. He had been living on the wings of her grace ever since using the equity in the home several times to cope with an unhappy life. Nick prayed to his ex-wife and asked for forgiveness. The thought of violating her memory made Nick sick to his stomach. Emotions and strong drink roiled within him until he vomited up his dinner.

It was only after Victoria had remarried that she became deathly ill. The doctors didn't know what the problem was. Something auto-immune disorder was dissolving her spinal tissue. After a year on a series of trial medications, she could no longer walk or stand. Nick often went to see her lying on what would eventually become her death bed. He remembered her looking so frail. He felt as if their marriage had sucked the marrow from her bones and all that was left lay before him. Her last words to Nick still haunted him. A week before her untimely end, he stopped by to read her favorite spy novel to her as he did every week. But on that night, she grabbed his hand with but an ounce of strength and whispered, "I never loved you the way you needed to be loved, Nick. I see that now and I am very sorry. Can you forgive me?" Nick couldn't believe his ears. He told her "yes", he had forgiven her and was about to ask for her forgiveness but quickly had to excuse himself. Nick had planned to make it to the bathroom down the hall but the pain of his ignorance, of his wife's absolute purity, crushed him. His knees slammed down onto the floor of the hospital corridor and he cried for the first time in his adult life. He cried so loud that the nurses had to pick him up and put him into an empty examination room. There he wept uncontrollably holding onto the legs of a cold metal chair. When he gathered himself, some twenty minutes later, he returned to Victoria's room only to find her peacefully resting. He kissed her on the forehead and left the room never to see her alive again.

The memory of that night played over in Nick's mind. It had been wearing a hole in his heart for quite some time. He was teetering very close to the edge of suicidal thoughts when a merciful sleep took hold of him. Warmed by the dying fire and his sleeping bag, Nick closed his eyes on a world that he still didn't fully understand.

The following morning came on like a freight train. Before Nick could get a fitful sleep it was time to pack up the campsite and move on. It was clear that Tommy had rested well. He gave Nick a look of concern when he saw the sallow expression on his face.

"You look like crap, man," Tommy observed shouldering his pack.

"Yeah, I kept the party going long after you passed out," Nick answered.

"Well, are you ready? We've got to push on through this canyon until it we reach the other side of the ridge."

"I'll manage. It won't be the first time I've had to work through a hangover."

"Drink some water. Here! I was saving this apple for my lunch, but you can have it now."

"Where did you get it?"

"You know me. I got all kinds of stuff I'm not telling you about."

Nick bit into the bright green Granny Smith. Its sharp, sweet flavors woke him up and helped settle his stomach. He washed it down with a bit too much from his canteen. After both men relieved themselves over the ashes of last night's flames, they started out eager for the day to begin. The two friends spent most of the morning articulating their thin frames around waist-tall boulders and thick beds of cacti. They met back up with the northern end of the same stream that flowed down to the creek bed where Tommy's Bronco was parked. This high up the water was colder and fresher. They took a moment to refill their canteens and share a cigarillo before walking another couple of miles to the canyon's rim. The view was spectacular. Lake Halmeth shimmered like a jade amulet off to the west. Windswept cumulus clouds glided north across the sky in concert. Their movement created an audible power like the voice of a great churning ocean.

"This is it. This is the place. I can feel the game before I even see 'em." Tommy raised his binoculars to his eyes expectantly. Satisfied with their location he passed them on to Nick. "Two pairs are better than one, my friend. Tell me if you see anything."

Nick grabbed the binoculars and set them against his tanned cheeks. He scanned the country but saw nothing of note. They were still too far out to differentiate the colors of the brush from those of beasts. For another hour they crept out onto several vantage points searching for prey. Finally, while embedded in a snaking row of rush, Nick spotted slight movement to the north at the base of a low-lying foothill a thousand meters ahead. Nick couldn't believe his luck. "Well, I got 'first sight'. There's a doe up there right at the base of where those two ridges meet. She's chewing her cud. Looks like she's alone."

Tommy snatched the binoculars away from Nick. He was flustered that he hadn't caught the sight himself. He scanned the area Nick had described and his mouth opened in wonder. "Well, I'll be damned, there she is all right. How do we get down there without spooking her?"

"I thought we were in line for bucks, Tommy? You wanna kill a doe before winter?" Nick believed it bad mojo to kill a doe when her fawns needed her most. He leveraged his understanding of the hunter's code against Tommy's desire for a full stomach.

"We're living in uncertain times, my friend. We need to kill everything we come across before winter sets in. Besides, if she's chewing her cud, it means she feels safe. There's bound to be others around her. I just can't see a clean approach."

"I'm rated at a thousand meters on a day like today. What about you?" Nick asked proudly.

"The same, but it's easy to miss a target at this distance. And even if we do zero in on her from this range the shot will ring out across the entire valley. Every deer within ten clicks will scatter."

"Well, what do you propose we do then?"

"We've got to make our way down to our left quietly and slowly. I mean we can't jostle nothing on our way down. We set up way down there by that stand of trees and wait for something bigger to come along. Then we bag as many as we can. I'll kill the deer since you seem to have so many emotions over the matter."

"Sounds good. Let's go."

The two friends started down the northwest side of the canyon's slope. It was blocked in by giant cliff faces littered with loose rock. Their silent descent took the better part of half an hour before they nested at the base of three Digger Pines. They had made out the run and instinctively knew that they were well in line with the herd's range. Sure enough, an hour after midday, a massive buck with shed horns came to the edge of the brush right where the doe had been. Tommy almost peed himself. Nick was happy. This buck could very well sate Tommy's lust for the hunt.

"Look at the size of that guy! It looks like a damn bull moose."

"Who's gonna get him?" Nick asked.

"I'll Roshambo you for it."

"Dammit. Alright." Nick pumped his fist three times and chose scissors. Tommy had somehow figured out how to read Nick's wrist muscles years ago and held his fist tight at the last moment.

"Ha. Uh-huh. Now you just sit back there and watch me tag this buck." Tommy was delighted in having the 'first kill', a good omen to any gamesman. "Don't worry, you can down the next one."

"Whatever. Just don't miss." Nick said focusing his attention downrange.

Tommy slowly crept into position, lined his sights on his target, and curled his right index around the cold metal trigger. As if on cue, rain began to fall. The two men craned their necks up at a dark grey thunderhead that had formed directly above them. The hunters didn't mind getting wet. They knew that rain gave deer cover and heightened their sense of safety. The buck was keeping himself busy rubbing his horns against the trunk of a cottonwood when Tommy took the shot. BANG! Nick, who had kept his reticle fixed on the stag, watched the majestic animal fall to the ground instantly. The rain muffled the shot beautifully. Tommy had placed the bullet directly in the base of the buck's neck. They could hear its last moans ebb out into the ether. Tommy jumped up holding his rifle in the air and ran over to his kill. Nick wrangled everything together and followed.

They were both almost out of breath by the time they reached their kill. Barely any blood had let from its wound. The buck's massive body was still warm.

"Wow, man. An eight-point buck! This is one of the finest stags I've nabbed in a long time. Eh, Nick, you're good luck, man." Tommy laughed.

"That was a really good shot. Your bullet went straight through its carotid artery. The heat from the round practically cauterized the bullet hole." Nick observed.

"You know, this guy's packing a lot of meat, man. I don't want to lose even an ounce. What say we take 'em back to the Bronco now and clean 'em."

"We should clean him when we get back to the cabin. It's too damp out here right now. We should definitely gut him soon, though."

"Alright, good call. We'll push further south than where we camped last night. But wherever we end up, we'll gut him good. C'mon. Let's get a move on. Time is not on our side anymore." Tommy exclaimed patting Nick on the back.

Nick was happy that Tommy had brought down such a big buck. The does would be safe for now. They constructed a litter from a couple of fallen maple branches and zip-tied the giant buck to it. The deadweight of the animal was tremendous, and they ended up having to untie the animal so that they could add cross member sections to their litter. That way they could holster the weight of the carcass using two shoulders instead of only one. Retracing their path proved a mammoth endeavor. They both gassed out at the top of the canyon. Tommy suggested an infusion of liquid courage might help them press on. Nick welcomed the hair of the dog and the two of them finished off the bottle of Jameson they had barely dented the night before.

Nick imagined the strength ancient hunters must have summoned to transport their kills. And that was after having chased down their prey and overpowering them with spears and knives. They passed through their old campsite and continued south following the ridgeline that had brought them to the canyon. Fueled by Irish whiskey and half a joint, the guys decided to trek it all the way back to the Bronco. Nick used every last bit of strength he had to make it back to the washed-out creek bed early the next morning. They dropped their prize in the boot of the Bronco and passed out in its spacious cab. The rain was still coming down in sheets. And provided the two hunters with the same sense of comfort and safety that the buck must have felt just before Tommy's bullet severed its spine. Too tired to dream, the two hunters slept heartily, content with their hunt and with their lives.

Chapter 3: Break

Leila's family had been waiting patiently in line for days. They had registered a week before the final deadline in Johannesburg and as a result, were part of a huge backlog of last-minute applicants. They along and some two thousand other people were sitting, sleeping, and leaning on top of stacked sandbags in a large tent subdivided by a dizzying system of electrified fencing. NATO troops were everywhere making sure that order was being maintained. Her family's experience of the collection center wasn't nearly as bad as many of the news reports had made them out to be. There were, however, occasional flare-ups but the blue bereted soldiers handled them promptly and with impunity. Leila was proud of her fellow South Africans for remaining relatively civil.

"Leila, eat your sandwich. We don't know when the next meal is coming." Her father, Richard, ordered in a firm but pleasant tone.

"Okay, fine." Leila hated ham sandwiches. The texture of the meat reminded her of rat tails. And the thought of rat tails grossed her out. She slyly removed the ham slice tossing it behind a stack of boxes and enjoyed her cheese, tomato, and mayonnaise on white bread. It was a little dry but tasted good going down.

"Richard, what is taking so long? Can't anything be done?" Leila's mother, Coffee, asked. "We've been sitting in the same spot for two days. Please go and ask them again." Coffee looked at Richard who was waiting for the 'magic' word. "Please."

"Of course, my love. But they will only tell me the same thing again." Richard promised. He turned and left disappearing into the cold heart of the fences, gates, and guards.

"What do you think they're going to tell him, Mom?" Leila asked.

"Something. Anything." Coffee groaned hands on her hips. Leila's mother was a corpulent Eritrean beauty. She had married Richard, a Welshman, against her parent's wishes. But when Leila was born and Coffee's parents saw how undeniably adorable their granddaughter was their hearts were forever changed. Leila was an only child but had twenty-four cousins and eight aunties and uncles who lived all over the world, and that was just on her mother's side. As a result, Leila was extremely well-traveled for a ten year-old. She had already touched her toes on every continent save Antarctica. Richard's family mostly lived in England. He had one brother, Dodd, who lived in the U.S., but no one ever talked to him. For this reason, Leila identified more with her mother's side of the family. The lanky Welshman returned after twenty minutes with a look of eternal patience.

Leila could tell by the sharp glint in her father's eyes that he had some kind of news.

"They told me they're waiting for the operations manager of this facility to return before they admit the last of us. They should be here sometime this afternoon." He explained with a measure of relief.

"Let's hope so. I am tired of waiting out here with all these bugs biting me." Coffee whined. "Why don't they bite you or Leila? I would feel better if they bit you, Richard."

"They like sweet things, my love."

"Stop it." Coffee laughed. "I am being attacked right now and you're making jokes."

"We told you to take the spray, Mom," Leila added her two cents. "But you don't like how it smells. So, it serves you right for always trying to be so fashionable."

"What? I am your mother. Where did you learn to talk like that to me?" Coffee pinched Leila on the fat of her upper arm.

69

"Ouch! What'd you do that for?" Leila screamed rubbing her arm.

"Because if no mosquitos will bite you, I will." Coffee teased. They all laughed together making light of an anxious situation.

"Maybe we should have gone to the collection center in Pretoria. I don't care for that place, but I should have considered it."

"No, I don't like Pretoria. I'd rather wait here." Coffee agreed. "I'm going to get some bottled water for us and stretch my legs, okay. I'll be back."

"Okay." Leila chimed.

"How are you doing, pumpkin?" Richard asked his little girl.

"I'm fine. How are you?" Leila laughed. "You look tired, daddy."

"I am sweetie. You know I had to come straight from the storage unit when I picked you and your mother up. I haven't had a chance to get any sleep since we arrived here."

"Take a nap. Don't worry. There are soldiers everywhere. Mommy and I will protect you." Leila said in a tone similar to her mother's. Richard felt okay with his daughter's suggestion. And, if he napped while Coffee was a way she would not wake him upon her return.

"Okay. But if anything changes, even the weather, you will wake me up, won't you?"

"Of course," Leila promised. She laid out a blanket on top of a stack of sandbags and made a little pillow for her dad out of her balled up sweater.

"Thank you, love. Make sure you tell your mother that this was all your idea. I don't want her getting short with me." He smiled.

"Go to sleep, dad." Richard closed his eyes and in seconds was in dreamland.

It didn't take long for Coffee to return with five water bottles, two more than her tiny family was allotted. When she saw her husband sleeping she gave Leila a sly smirk. The young girl just looked at her mother and giggled. There was nothing either of her parents could do to fight against Leila's charms. They weren't easy parents, by any means, but Leila had a way of disarming people. Coffee liked to think it was because her daughter genuinely loved people. But it was more than that, Leila's very being seemed to represent a new, brighter world, a world where racism, sexism, and poverty were distant memories of a nightmarish past.

"I see you let your dad get some rest, huh? It's okay, he's earned some sleep."

"Everybody needs sleep, mom. You don't earn it."

"Not in my family. Everyone must work, even you little girl." Coffee tried to pinch Leila again but wasn't quick enough.

"Mom, what will happen to all those people we saw in Soweto?" Leila changed the mood of the conversation.

"I don't know. There are millions of people like that all over the world. The government only has room for citizens, not those who are here illegally. We almost weren't allowed to be here either, remember. We had to get the British embassy to permit us to enter the shelters here. The line between who has rights as a citizen and who doesn't is very thin."

"But when the storms come all those people are going to die, right?"

"I suppose some of them will. But I have a feeling many will survive. Look, sweetie, it took me a whole week to convince your dad that we should register here in Johannesburg. He didn't want to go. He wanted to take us to go live in the Welsh countryside with his aunt. I told him 'no way'. So, there are many families just like ours that have chosen not to go underground."

"What?" Leila pouted throwing her hands up in the air, "I would have liked to live in the countryside. You didn't even ask me."

"Please, child, there would be nothing for you to do in the countryside but work. Do you know how to split logs for the fire or defrock a rooster for supper?"

"No."

"What exactly do you think you would be doing up there aside from working your little fingers to the bone, huh? What?"

"I could play...out in the forest and ride horses."

"Horses? You have never so much as asked me about horses before today. You are being silly. Look, when you are a mommy, you can choose what is best for your own family, okay. But I am the mother of this family. You must listen to me. That's how it goes."

"You should have at least told me."

"Well, maybe you're right, Leila. I'm sorry. I see now that I made a mistake. Okay?" Coffee asked for her daughter's forgiveness. Leila knew the circumstances must have been extraordinary because she had rarely ever heard her mother say she was sorry for anything.

"Okay, but I don't want to eat any more ham sandwiches. Daddy makes me eat them and I hate them. I'd rather just eat the bread and the tomato."

"Alright, no more ham sandwiches. Come here, baby." Coffee held out her thick strong arms and they hugged out their differences.

They sat together for a few hours playing card games with each other while Richard slept peacefully. But as they finished up their umpteenth round of gin rummy the tented complex began to shake. Great gusts of wind from the eastern edge of the collection center whirled through the tent sending debris and people's documents skittering about everywhere. The sound of heavy helicopter rotors chopping through the humid air filled Leila's ears.

"Mom, what is that?"

Coffee didn't answer. She immediately turned to wake Richard. He pushed himself up and got to his feet. Without rubbing the sleep from his eyes, he told his family to pack up their cards because the line would be moving soon.

"This must be the person the guards spoke of," Richard yelled over the sound of the giant helicopter which was longer than a school bus.

Leila wanted to get a better view and asked her dad if he could put her on his shoulders. He obliged. He and Leila, along with everyone else in line, looked to see who was to emerge from the helicopter. Unfortunately, the view of the helipad was blocked by the aluminum fencing that formed the perimeter of the collection center. Leila trained her eyes instead on the entrance into the facility that the occupants of the helicopter would most likely use, which was in full view. The line began to move and people's attention became focused on what was ahead of them and not behind. Leila, still on her father's shoulders, couldn't seem to take her eyes off the door closest to the helicopter. Finally, she saw a small army of soldiers escort a very tall person shrouded in a heavy black cloak toward the very door Leila had been fixated on. In a split second, which seemed like an eternity, the hooded figure turned its head and from across a great span stared directly into Leila's eyes. She instantly became horrified. Before she could say or do anything whatever had just captured her gaze disappeared into the underground complex along with the military escort. Leila started to absorb what she had just seen. The images played together in her mind's eye piercing her subconscious like a hot knife through butter. Whatever it was had yellow eyes with thin black pupils. Leila had no frame of reference for the creature she had witnessed. All she could relate it to were the demons mentioned in the Bible. Within a matter of seconds Leila's fears of Hell and the Devil, coupled with the being's horrifying appearance, morphed into a series of shrill, gut-wrenching cries.

"Oh my God? What is wrong, Leila?" Richard picked her up off his shoulders and looked at his daughter. She refused to look at him. The image of the creature's face had superimposed itself upon her world. Everywhere she looked there it was, its yellow eyes staring back at her. Leila bawled uncontrollably pointing in the direction of the door the creature had gone into.

"Baby, what is the matter?" Coffee asked. It had been years since she had seen her daughter consumed in such a fit of hysteria. It was extremely out of character for the otherwise mature ten year-old. Both parents knew something was wrong. They continued to try to console their daughter who started to kick and scream as the line crept forward. Leila simply refused to go any further. People in line, sensing the uncontrollable fear they all harbored deep down, began to look around for clues as to what had upset the little girl. Not seeing anything of note, they assumed Leila's behavior was the product of bad parenting and began to scold Coffee and Richard openly and without shame.

"Let me handle my own family. You just worry about your own!" Richard barked at a group of hecklers who accused him of not knowing how to parent his child. The strength in his voice startled even his wife. "Leila, listen to me very carefully. I need you to calm down so that you can tell me what happened."

Coffee stroked Leila's wavy fawn-colored hair to soothe the troubled youth.

"Please, baby, just tell us what happened." Coffee pleaded.

"Th-there's a m-m-monster inside. I saw it. It came from the helicopter." Leila managed between sobs. Her body quivered at the remembrance of how the creature moved. Its limbs seemed to twitch and jerk about. "We can't go in there, daddy! We can't go. Don't make me go in there! We can't go in there. Don't make me go! Please, momma. Please!"

Coffee looked at Richard with wide eyes not understanding what to make of their daughter's troubled visions. The line moved forward again several feet. Leila felt as though her body was being sucked into a menacing black hole. She fell to the ground using her prone bodyweight like an anchor. She consciously put her parents in the position of having to lose face in front of a crowd of people if she did not get her way. Coffee caught on to her child's clever tactic and became incensed, emboldened to resolve the matter. There was no way for her, not seeing the creature Leila had, to understand the intentions of her flesh and blood.

Coffee was no fool. She had prepared for this scenario without telling Richard anything about it. She hadn't thought Leila would be so stubborn about the registration process but she did expect her daughter to be a little apprehensive.

"Richard, please go into my purse and hand me the green pills that are in the orange container." Coffee asked authoritatively. Richard looked at his wife knowing what she intended. It was obvious he did not agree. Coffee's temper flared. "Richard, just hand me the damn pills!"

Without another word, Richard did as his wife commanded. He also brought bottled water and handed the items to his wife in disgust. Coffee's eyes were like those of a Great White Shark, coal-black and brimming with a naturally bred determination. At that moment, her will was absolute. She took three of the pills and put her eyes once more on her husband. "Hold her."

Richard held his daughter's arm's as she flailed against him. He regarded his wife coldly as she jammed the pills down their daughter's throat. And when Leila refused to swallow them Coffee plugged the little girl's nose forcing the pills down. When the deed had been done someone in the line behind them clapped in approval. Coffee threw her gaze at the woman who withdrew grinning like a mischievous coward. It was the most unpleasant moment they had ever experienced as a family. Within minutes, Leila became despondent. Richard looked into his daughter's beautiful eyes and shed a quiet tear. He picked her up in his arms and rocked her like a newborn.

When it was their turn to approach one of the many registration desks they were summoned forward by a woman whose face appeared to have been carved from stone. Coffee approached without the slightest hesitation. Her husband, still holding Leila, reluctantly followed.

"Proof of citizenship." The registrar ordered. Coffee thrust a folder filled with papers into the registrar's face. The registrar, realizing she had met her match in terms of strength of character, eyed the small family with a notable amount of empathy. "I commend you for the way you handled that situation. I know it is not easy for a mother to do what is necessary when so many others are watching." Coffee simply nodded her head. Her shoulder's relaxed a little, something her husband thankfully noticed.

"Where is your embassy's letter of recommendation for registration?" the registrar asked. Coffee furnished it unflinchingly.

"Good. Everything is in order. Now all I need to see is proof of income for the last ten years."

At this request, Richard stepped forward. "I have only the last seven."

"Fine." The woman replied coldly obviously viewing Richard's noncompliance as incompetence. She reviewed the documents sternly pouring over the numbers like a shrewd accountant. "You are a professor at the University?"

"Yes. I teach Comparative Literature." Richard said proudly.

"You don't earn enough." The registrar stamped their collection application with a big stamp that read, 'POP-C'. She handed the document to Richard without looking up. "You're done here. Please move your family forward into the line marked by the red arrows on the floor."

"What does 'POP-C' mean?" Richard asked desperately feeling altogether disrespected.

The registrar looked up at Richard as though he were but a child and said, "It means you are going into a general population shelter with everyone else in your income bracket. Is there a problem? I trust you have already made your decision. There are 2000 other people behind you, sir. So, please, move on."

Coffee grabbed her husband and pulled him forward toward the appropriate line.

"This isn't right." Richard pointed out to his wife. "They are housing people according to their income levels, Coffee. Maybe we should rethink this." Richard prepared for his wife to lash out at him. He was surprised when she did not. She turned to him and quietly cried into his side.

Richard couldn't put his arms around his wife as Leila was still in them. The line they were now in moved much faster than the previous one. As they pushed forward Coffee looked up at Richard through tears and kissed him.

"I am sorry, Richard." Coffee apologized leaning on his shoulder. It was the most subtle way anyone could have ever ended a heated disagreement. Richard didn't say anything. It was clear that the matter of force-feeding pills to their child was no longer up for debate. Leila began to stir like a toddler wanting to walk. Richard let her down softly and the three of them stepped over the line that demarcated the entrance to the underground shelter. Leila didn't make a sound. She just looked around the giant building in awe holding her father's hand. The opening to the underground facility was about as wide as a football pitch was long. It jutted out of the ground like some giant exhaust vent. Its ceiling was 30 feet tall and the entire structure was made of solid concrete. The red arrows they had been following went straight into the mouth of the structure while two other lines, one marked in green, the other blue, veered off to the right and left. There were significantly more people in the POP-C line than in the other two. The small family came to a point in the line where they could see its terminus. At its end, two large garage doors, halfway raised, sat side by side. They were separating genders for some reason. Richard rifled through the registration papers they had been given and realized there was a short explanation of the process through which they were now undergoing.

"It says here that they are going to decontaminate everyone separately according to sex. They will conduct a cavity search and a routine medical exam before they allow us inside the shelters." Coffee didn't say anything. She just squeezed Richard's hand in acknowledgment of his words.

When it came time for them to be separated Richard made sure that they were to be housed in the same shelter. They were assured that it was so. Richard, satisfied, sought kisses from the two loves of his life before ducking under the doorway into the men's examination room. Coffee and Leila followed suit entering the room on the left. Two female nurses were inside waiting for them decked head to toe in long-sleeved scrubs and surgical masks.

"Ma'am, what is wrong with your child?" one of the nurses asked through her disposable face mask. She probed Leila's dilated pupils with a penlight.

"I had to give her medicine to calm her down." Coffee admitted feeling guilty.

"What did you give her and how much?"

"1200mgs of Vicodin." Coffee started shaking and cried at the sound of her cruelty. She handed the nurse the bottle of pills.

"Ma'am, it's okay. You are not the first person to have to sedate their child. In about twelve hours the Vicodin will be free of her system, okay?" the nurse assured her. "But I will have to take your medicine. I am sorry. We have your medical records. Any prescription you will need will be administered by our staff. Is that clear?"

"I don't understand. How did you obtain our medical records?"

"Your embassy sent them to us when you applied for registration here in Gauteng." The nurse answered.

"Oh, okay." Coffee answered still not sure how that information had been forwarded without their permission.

"Now listen to me very carefully. I don't have time to repeat myself or argue over this next issue. But you must release your child into my care so that we can decontaminate her separately. Do you understand and comply?"

"Yes, I understand."

"Do you comply?"

"Yes, I comply." Coffee didn't see why they had to use such a forceful word. It was disingenuous, to say the least.

"Nurse Oliver, would you please escort..." the nurse took another look at the medical records on her computer monitor, "please, escort Leila to decontamination bay 209?"

"Certainly." The larger, younger nurse took Leila by the hand and led her through a doorway beyond the sight of her mother who could only look on, pain saddling around her face. The nurse took Leila through a darkened corridor and placed her in an empty room that had a conveyor belt in the middle of the floor. She then knelt beside the conveyor and looked into Leila's glassy eyes. "Now, Leila, I want you to step on this people mover and stay still. Don't move at all no matter what. We want to make sure you don't have any bugs hiding in your pretty hair, okay? Pretty soon this will be all over. Will you do that for me? Now, I need to put you in this medical gown so that the machines won't have a problem scanning your body."

Leila shook her head and allowed the nurse to strip her of her jeans, shoes, and t-shirt. She then fit Leila with an all-white hospital gown that hung below her knees. The nurse turned on the conveyor using a remote. Leila was slowly brought into another room where her body was scanned by a few different medical devices. A green light shone brightly from above her signaling the completion of the examination. The conveyor belt started to move again taking Leila into another room that was sealed off from the others. The belt stopped her just in front of a large monitor that began to play a prerecorded message explaining the rules of conduct expected of all citizens inside the shelters. Leila heard none of it. Her eyes blurred the image on the screen. She could only tell that there was a woman dressed in military uniform saying something in an upbeat monotone voice. When the video stopped playing the floor opened up underneath Leila's feet. She tumbled into a sparsely lit tunnel that descended sharply like a water slide. After sliding a great distance her body was ejected into a great cavernous room filled with hundreds of other people. Leila slowly got to her feet and looked around. She couldn't make heads or tails of what she was seeing. People came up to her to try to help but she refused their advances and went off to sit by herself. Having finally made it to the shelter, Leila's will could no longer hold out against the power of the pills. She passed out unaware that her mother and father were nowhere to be found.

Chapter 4: Close Encounter

Tommy took the drive home nice and slow not wanting to disturb the cargo in the back of the Bronco. He was high energy after such a short, successful hunt. Nick was still falling in and out of sleep in the passenger seat when Tommy turned onto the road that led to the cabin. The slow bumpy ride forced Nick to sit up straight and wipe the sleep from his eyes. Their testosterone-filled hump the day before had taken more out of Nick than it had Tommy, who had always somehow kept himself in better shape even though he never exercised. When they reached the cabin Tommy backed up to his garage and got out. Nick followed not looking forward to muscling their kill out of the boot. Nick opened the tailgate while Tommy raised the garage door. They were about to get knee deep in blood and hide when Tommy stopped in his tracks.

"Hmm. That's weird." Tommy noted.

"What?" Nick asked.

"I don't hear Jasper. He usually barks whenever I come home."

"He's probably just asleep with Arnold," Nick suggested.

"Do me a favor? Go check the house for me." Tommy requested tossing his keys to his best friend.

"Yeah, sure thing." Nick flew up the stairs to the front door even though he was still a little sleepy. He unlocked the door expecting to see Arnold greet him excitedly. But when Nick checked the few rooms of the house neither he nor Jasper were inside. Nick went out to the backyard thinking that both dogs might be soaking in the late morning sun. It was empty. He called out to Arnold but there was no response. Nick became confused as to what exactly was happening. Where the hell were their dogs? He checked around the property for holes in the fence but found nothing unusual until he went to the side of the house. The gated entrance to the backyard had been broken into. Whoever had done it had sawed out the portion of the gate that housed the latch and lock with a Sawz-All. Nick ran back out to the garage where Tommy had already cherry-picked the stag and had placed it onto a sturdy metal folding table for cleaning.

"Tommy! The dogs are gone, man. Somebody broke in through the side gate."

"What? Are you serious?" Tommy stopped what he was doing and followed Nick to the side of the house calling Jasper's name the whole time. He inspected the cut in the gate cursing at length.

"I know who did this," Tommy growled.

"It's that crazy old bum, isn't it?"

"The one and only. I'm breaking out the big guns for this. Come on, I know where that bastard lives. I hope he's not doing what I think he's doing with our friggin' dogs, so help me God I'll kill him. I'll dissect the son of a bitch." Tommy promised as the two men ran down to the cellar. Tommy grabbed an M-5 and a 9mm semi-automatic pistol. Nick grabbed a Mossberg 12 gauge and stuffed it full of shot. He grabbed a small HK as well and concealed it in the small of his back.

They returned to the Bronco and sped off leaving their kill exposed and the garage door open. Tommy flew down the fire road and before it ended stopped to engage the four-wheel drive. He made a sharp left turn and started tearing up the hill away from the road. Tommy drove his truck like a rally car narrowly missing several skinny pines as he muttered curse words under his breath. Nick could see his friend's rage fomenting like a pressure cooker. Had Tommy listened to him about the old man maybe the situation could have been avoided. But Nick knew better than to say, "I told you so". Tommy would have undoubtedly overreacted to the opportunistic dig. Tommy kept driving until he came to the top of the hill. He parked the Bronco in front of what appeared to be an old abandoned mine shaft complete with steel tracks and a sign that read, 'Danger. Enter At Your Own Risk.'

"You gotta be kidding me? Where is my damn dog, Tommy?" The ridiculousness of the situation infuriated Nick who had up until that point remained relatively quiet.

"Beggar's Mine. Everyone knows he squats in here. The teenagers who used to smoke pot up here would see him all the time. Dale! Come out here right now!" Tommy yelled through the military issue megaphone attached to the top of his truck. He honked his horn repeatedly but there was no response. Tommy looked at Nick. "We're going in. Grab that flashlight in the glove box. I've got a flood lamp in the back. Let's go."

Nick grabbed the mag lite and the two men stormed into the mine's entrance. Tommy shined his handheld flood light into the shaft which was tall enough for a man to walk slightly stooped. The shaft stretched forward some two hundred yards until teeing off. When they came to the tee they decided to both go left. They kept on for some time until they heard the sound of sliding rocks.

"Dale, is that you? We won't hurt you. Just give us back our dogs, man! Right now! Stop screwing with me, Dale. I'm not playing around." Tommy shouted cocking back the hammer of his pistol.

"How can this guy see in here without any light?" Nick asked astounded.

"Who knows? He probably can't and just doesn't care." Tommy answered.

"Arnold! Arnold!" Nick got the idea to call out for his bulldog. He heard a faint bark off in the distance. "Wait. Wait. Shhh. Did you hear that? That's Arnold, man." Nick held his breath for a moment. "Come on. Hurry!"

"How on God's green earth did you even hear that?" Tommy asked amazed at Nick's ability to focus on the slightest noise coming from some inner chamber in the shaft up ahead.

"Come on, this way!" Nick took the lead walking briskly, clearing section after section. Nick continued calling after his dog who barked in return sensing his rescue was nigh. The two men came to a section of the tunnel that had caved in. There was only enough room at the top for them to squeeze through on all fours. They could see an eerie red light shining from the other side of the collapsed rock.

"Dammit, Dale! Pain in my ass." Tommy complained as he went through the opening first disappearing over the other side. Nick followed behind as fast as he could. When Nick climbed down the other side Arnold began to whine at the sight of his master. Tommy had his handgun aimed at Dale who, in turn, had a butcher knife to Arnold's throat. The stout bully was chained to a section of broken steel track on the ground.

"I should've shot you when I had the chance, old man! Lower the knife, Dale!" Nick said with mortal authority.

"Heehee. I ain't scared of dying." Dale wheezed. "What brings y'all to this neck of the woods?"

"Where is Jasper, Dale?" Tommy yelled. Dale just laughed before cocking his head to the side listening to the silence. Tommy fired a shot off near Dale's head. But the old man simply giggled and pushed the edge of the butcher knife a little deeper into Arnold's neck. Arnold winced in pain.

Nick had had enough and fired three successive shots. The first bullet tore into Dale's elbow causing the old man to drop the blade. The second bullet flew through Dale's left knee dropping him to the ground. And the final shot shattered the chain that held Arnold, who immediately ran to Nick in relief. Nick knelt down and allowed his buddy to lick him all over the face. Dale was in a great deal of pain but managed to stand up again, cackling and mumbling to himself the whole time.

"Where is the other dog, Dale? Where's Jasper?" Tommy closed in on the old man and punched the snot out of him. Dale spit blood out of his mouth and tried to put up a fight but didn't have the strength to free himself from Tommy's clutches. "Talk goddamit!"

"Look, you don't get it. No, you don't get it." Dale said rubbing his head. His emaciated body could be seen through the rips in the man's clothes. "I must feed him. He must eat. That's my job, y'know. I find food for him."

"What are you talking about?" Tommy grilled Dale shaking him like a paint can.

"The big brown one. What was that sucker, a Great Dane, or somethin'? Heehee. Yeah, he's dead...he's gone, pal. He made quick work of that one."

"My dog is dead?" Tommy looked at Nick, anger, and loss crinkling his face. Nick could tell Tommy was about to kill the old man. "Who killed my dog, Dale? Just tell me. I'm going to kill you, either way, you know that, don't you?" Tommy assured the old man. Dale did nothing but lift his finger pointing it down the shaft to his right.

"Whatever's left...is in there," Dale whispered, his words barely audible. Tommy had to put his ear to the man's mouth to hear him. He flung Dale to the ground and rushed down the shaft pointing his floodlight ahead of him.

"Tie his dumbass up, Nick. Then take Arnold and get outta here. You're not going to want to see what I do to him." Tommy ordered before disappearing around a wall of rock at the end of the tunnel.

"Ouch. Owww. Haha." Dale squealed as Nick tied his neck to the same rail Arnold had been chained to. "You're friend ain't gonna like what he has to see."

"If I were you I would gather my thoughts, old man. They will be your last." Nick said feeling sorry for the guy who obviously suffered from a host of psychological disorders. He took Arnold, climbed the rock wall, and began squeezing through its gap. Arnold made it through long before his master. Once on the other side, Nick heard Tommy's muffled cries in the adjacent shaft as he, no doubt, discovered Jasper's remains. Nick kept on. Tommy had been right. Even though Dale deserved to die, Nick didn't want to witness him torture the old man. When Nick had almost reached the entrance to the mine he heard a series of shots ring out from the inner workings of the mine. He was surprised that Nick had finished Dale off so quickly. Nick opened the cab of the Bronco and helped Arnold jump up and into the front seat. They waited there for Tommy who was bound to be pretty shaken up when he returned.

Tommy finally made it out of the mine but was not the same. He was carrying Jasper's bloodied remains inside his jacket. Tommy placed the bundle of blood and bones in the back of his truck and then got into the driver's seat. The two friends remained silent the whole way home. After Tommy pulled up to his cabin he hopped out and immediately grabbed a shovel from the garage. He carried Jasper's dead body to the backyard slamming the side gate behind him even though he knew it wouldn't shut. Nick decided to let Tommy be and led Arnold through the front door and brought his bowl of food out for him. Arnold ate heartily and lapped up more water than Nick had ever seen him drink. He watched Tommy digging Jasper's grave from the kitchen window. He wished there was something he could do. Nick contemplated packing up his stuff into his pickup and leaving right then but something told him he should stay. He sat down on the couch and decided to take a nap. Arnold plopped next to him and before long they were both asleep.

When he woke up the sun had already set leaving behind a mauve sky. All the lights in the cabin were off. Tommy was sitting across from Nick watching him sleep, the failing light of dusk the only light in the room.

"How'd you sleep, Nick?" Tommy asked sarcastically.

"I thought you might need some space." Nick sat up. "Look, Tommy, I'm sorry about J..."

"You didn't kill my friggin' dog, Nick. I'm not mad at you. I'm pissed off. But I'm not pissed off at you. I'm glad Arnold is okay."

"Happy to hear it. I wasn't sure how you going to react to, well, whatever this is. Why are all the lights off?" Nick looked around knowing something was going on.

"What do you think Dale was talking about?" asked Tommy.

"I have no clue. It was all crazy talk."

"Yeah, well, I, for one, intend to find out."

"And how exactly are you gonna do that?"

"There were claw marks all over my dog, Nick. They were deep and their number and position matched those prints you showed me the other day."

"There's no way you can know that for sure." Nick countered.

"Which is why I have laid a trap for whatever it was that killed Jasper." Tommy motioned his head outside.

"The buck?"

"I strung him up by the side of the house. I've got three motion-sensing lights aimed at it. Whatever killed Jasper will go for it, for sure." Tommy stood up and put his hands in his jeans pockets. "Will you help me?"

"Of course, man. I mean, c'mon. You know you don't have to ask." Nick got up and gave his friend a much needed embrace.

"I'm gonna wait for it on the roof with my rail gun."

"What? A rail gun?" Nick chuckled. "Where in the hell did you get one of those?" Tommy didn't answer implying that Nick's line of questioning was not just an underestimation but an insult. "Okay, forget about it. Where do you want me?"

"Right here. I already cut a circle out of that glass in that window. It's large enough for a high caliber muzzle. I want you to use something big, something that this friggin' thing will feel. When whatever it is goes for the bait it will get lit up like a Christmas tree during a lightning storm. I want you to pump every last bit of lead you have into it."

"What do you we do about Arnold?" Nick asked knowing the overprotective bulldog might bark again if his nose gets tipped off.

"Hmm. Yeah, I guess just put him in the bathroom and shut the door. We should get ready now. I have some snuff if you think it'll help you focus." Tommy offered pulling a small round tin from his back pocket.

"No, I'm good. That stuff is gross." Nick replied.

"Suit yourself," Tommy said snorting a pinch of the mentholated powder. Nick shuddered at the sound.

The two men set everything up. Tommy got into position on the roof and radioed Nick to make sure their earpieces were on the right channel and set at the correct volume. Nick put Arnold in the bathroom and gave him a slice of frozen cow femur from Tommy's fridge to keep him busy. Nick chose to use an HK416 with a high-capacity magazine. He pushed the cushy arm of the couch perpendicular to the window and laid on it. After placing his muzzle through the opening in the window, Nick unfolded a small modular tripod that he had attached to the rifle's front end then radioed Tommy, "10-23?"

"Copy that. 10-12." Tommy answered using the police code for 'stand-by'.

The hunters waited in their positions for an hour. The sky was dark, and the cabin was shrouded in the blackness of night. It was so quiet Nick could hear his heartbeat. He began to recall being in a similar position while on a mission close to the Pakistani border. He wasn't a sniper but had often used a similar pincer position to neutralize hard targets who rarely showed themselves out in the open. Multiple vantage points exponentially reduced a target's options for escape or cover.

Nick did his best to keep his sights on the flayed stag but all he could think about were Dale's words. They hadn't made any sense at all. There was no way to know what kind of animal they were baiting. Nick refocused his thoughts back to his beating heart. He sat in silence for another twenty minutes when all of a sudden he heard faint scuffling noises on the roof coming from the opposite direction from where he knew Tommy was positioned. Nick trained his ears again this time hearing a definite creak caused by something heavy. Images of the deeply embedded footprints from underneath the cabin's window flashed through Nick's mind.

"Tommy, there's something on the roof. Turn around there's something up there with you!" Nick yelled into his earpiece.

"What?" Tommy answered. "Holy shit! Aaaahh!" Tommy screamed. Nick could only hear gunshots firing above him. Two bullets came whizzing through the roof almost striking Nick in the leg. Arnold began to bark loudly making it that much harder for Nick to concentrate. The motion sensor lights sprung on and Nick poised himself for a kill shot. But it was Tommy who had set off the motion sensors. He had been thrown off the roof by something. The lights flooded his battered body with pale green light.

"Tommy, what's going on?" Nick mistakenly yelled through the window giving away his position. Tommy put his hands up to his eyes shielding himself from the glare of the lights that beamed down upon him.

"Run! Nick, get the hell out of here!" Tommy shouted. One by one, the motion lights were being broken by whoever was on the roof. When the last one shattered the darkness returned and with it a great uncertainty. "Whoa. Whoa! Shoot Dammit. Nick, shoot. It's coming! Aagh!"

Nick let off a flurry of shots in Tommy's general direction knowing that he might kill the only friend he had in the world. Nick heard a deep growl and a long raspy utterance. He trained in on the origin of the noise and unloaded his entire magazine.

"AAARRGGH!" a brutal voice howled into the night air.

Nick heard the tethers that held the deer carcass snapping and flying off wildly. He was now out of ammo and had to get closer. He pulled himself from the window and ran to the bathroom to let Arnold out. Nick had to use the dog's nose as a lookout betting that Arnold would do a better job than he had done for Tommy. Nick heard a loud banging outside. Something was trying to break through the metal garage door. Arnold went running outside but stopped at the top of the stairs that led to the driveway begging for Nick to follow. By the time Nick made it outside the banging had stopped, but whatever had fled the scene could be heard ripping flesh apart from around the side of the cabin. Nick could barely make out the flank of the stag sticking out from around the house. Its muscles jerked as something gnawed on it ravenously. Nick gestured for Arnold to stay put and quickly scaled the stair railing pulling himself onto the roof of the house. He silently made his way to where Tommy had been earlier before being thrown off. His rail gun still lay at the edge of the roof. Nick picked it up ever so slightly careful not to let its bipod snap back into place at the sides of the forward lands. Whatever was down there was still chewing on the dear carcass. He fired a single shot at too close of range and was startled at the high-powered rifle's blowback. He lost sight of his target who was now wailing in pain. The sound of chewing had stopped. Nick could hear the animal moving slowly toward the front of the house. Arnold started barking again. Nick traced the animal's movements by walking to the side of the roof over the garage. His line of sight passed over the roof's edge and Nick finally caught a glimpse of his target. Nick couldn't believe his eyes. The creature had stepped fully into the light shining down from the front door. It was a seven-foot-tall monster so aggressive in its appearance that Nick almost crapped his pants. It was covered in its own blood which was dark blueish in color. Upon seeing Nick, it hunched down baring its teeth, fresh sinew still hanging from them. Nick ditched the rail gun and trained his .45mm at the creature's head but it didn't wait around for Nick to shoot. It ducked underneath the lip of the eaves and made its way over to the stairs toward Arnold. Nick jumped off the roof firing his handgun at the same time. The large reptilian being fell to its knees halfway up the stairs. Arnold, sensing an opportunity, launched himself at the creature's neck biting down on its jugular and locking his jaw. The blood curdled cries of the giant lizard bellowed through the night. The weight of the muscular bulldog carried through its jump and sent the creature's body twisting backward down the stairs. Despite being bruised and battered, Arnold had not let go and was still trying ardently to break the monster's neck. The creature clawed at Arnold leaving bloody gashes in the bully's white coat. Nick didn't want Arnold to share in Jasper's fate and yelled commands to him at the top of his lungs.

"Release! Heel." He yelled. "Release Dammit. Come over here now, Arnold!" The bulldog let go and heftily clambered down the stairs to his master's feet. Nick then ordered him to stay put. Nick turned his attention back to the creature who was badly mangled and lay at the foot of the stairs breathing heavily unable to move. He walked up to it with wide eyes beholding its awesome presence. The creature's face held within its composition such intelligence and calculated intention that Nick began to feel sorry for it. In that fleeting moment of empathy, the creature grabbed Nick's throat with one hand and clawed his face with the other. Then, in a final act of pure hatred and volatility, the lizardman spat a stream of hot, steaming mucus into the cuts it had opened in Nick's face. Nick screamed in pain as the stinky substance burned into his flesh giving off an odor that was as putrid as it was pungent. In disgust, the creature stared Nick straight in his eyes and spoke a language that didn't sound like anything Nick had ever heard.

"Erh tat drah gohn!" It spoke. Nick was overwhelmed by the madness of the scene and decided to end it. He raised his handgun firing five shots into the creature's open mouth. The monster's head flew back against the wooden staircase. Blue blood spattered everywhere. A final gasp of air reluctantly issued from the reptilian's body and its muscular limbs went limp.

Cracks of thunder began to roll through the open sky which lit up here and there with sudden sparks of lightning. A gentle rain followed anointing the hunters in a cascade of warm water. Nick grabbed his face, gun in hand. It was as if someone had splashed battery acid on him. He could barely see through one eye. What had the creature done to him? He felt nauseous and disoriented. He crashed against the dented garage door and slid to the ground. Arnold sat down next to Nick and licked his master's hand. The pair of them stayed there for a while watching the raindrops bounce off the dead creature's steaming body thankful to be alive.

The scales that covered the dorsal side of the reptilian appeared shiny, almost metallic. Its abdomen was shielded with larger, more flexible, flesh-colored plating. The monster's eyes, still open, were mustard yellow with black pinpricks for pupils surrounded by orange speckles. It was powerfully built and its physique, apart from its feet and ankles, resembled that of a human. The creature was something straight out of a comic book. It wore nothing except a herringbone codpiece that looked as though it had been made using a kind of woven metallic fabric. Dale was right, Nick thought to himself. There was no way anybody would have believed him. The creature was a bloody nightmare. Where had it come from? Was it an alien or some crazy government experiment? Nick heard Tommy calling for help from the low hill on the side of the house. He had totally forgotten about him. Arnold perked up and ran over to where Tommy lay.

"Tommy, I'm coming. Hold on, man. I'm right here." Nick screamed ambling awkwardly like a drunkard. "Tommy, where are you?" Arnold barked once as if to answer Nick's question.

"Over here!" Tommy could barely move. When Nick got to him Tommy had propped himself up against a tree covered in mud and blood. Arnold licked the crud off Tommy's face happy to see a friend.

"It's dead, Tommy. Whatever the hell it was, we killed it." Nick proclaimed. "Can you walk?"

"No, man. I can't feel my damn legs, Nick." Tommy winced. He sounded as though he was on the verge of crying. "I can't move my legs."

"What? What happened?"

"That thing threw me against this tree, man. I felt something inside me snap but I can't be sure where or what it was."

"C'mon. I'll help you up. You have got to see this friggin' thing otherwise you're never gonna believe it." Nick assured him.

"It was smart as a whip, Nick." Tommy pointed out. "It knew we were baiting it. How is that possible?"

"I don't know, Tommy," Nick replied. "But I'm freaked out. We're extremely lucky to be alive."

"I guess Dale wasn't so crazy after all, huh?"

"No, Dale was crazy alright." Nick found a little humor to lighten the mood. He brought Tommy to the reptilian's body and sat him next to it. Nick ran to grab a plastic lawn chair from the side of the house and when he returned, he sat Tommy in it.

"My God. Look at it. That is, hands down, the craziest thing I have ever seen in my life. It looks like a damn velociraptor/human hybrid. It hunts, kills, and can tell when it's being hunted, the perfect predator." Tommy thought aloud. "Did you see how it took out those lights?"

"It's worse than that, Tommy," Nick added looking into the creature's dead eyes with a flashlight.

"What do you mean?"

"It spoke to me. I am sure of it. Not in any language I know of, but it spoke words. The creature was intelligent, perhaps more intelligent, or at least more physically capable than you or I."

"I see it scratched the crap out of you, too," Tommy noted observing the grievous injury done to Nick's face. "And all these years I thought you were a pretty boy."

"It burns, man. We've got to clean our wounds, but I don't feel safe here."

"My head is pounding. And my legs..." Tommy looked up to the sky trying to hide his tears in the falling rain. He slammed his fists down on his numb thighs. He lowered his head down in acceptance.

"I need to get you to a doctor. But I have no idea where to go."

"We've got to do what we can here. Nowhere else is gonna have running water or electricity."

"Alright, but let's hurry up. I'm sorry but we need to find another place to live, man, unless you want to stay up here?"

"No, you're right. But I'm taking my guns with me."

"What are we going to do with that?" Nick asked his thumb gesturing toward the dead reptilian bleeding out on the gravel driveway."

"I'm taking that asshole's head. You can leave the rest of him here to rot, but the head's mine. Alright, help me up." Tommy said struggling. Nick put Tommy around him like a backpack and hoisted him up the stairs to the cabin while Arnold happily trailed behind them. Nick flicked the lights on in the house and brought Tommy into the bathroom where he began to run a bath for him. Like a battlefield nurse, Nick unabashedly helped undress his friend. He was relieved to see that Tommy's wounds, apart from a couple of deep scratches, had been relegated to his lower spine. Purple bruising ran up and down the small of Tommy's back. While bathing him Nick noticed that he most likely had a couple of broken ribs as well.

"Alright, Nurse Hackett, you've done your job. Now get the hell out." Tommy joked. He was in good spirits considering the circumstances. As Nick walked out of the bathroom, he glanced at himself in the fogged up vanity. After wiping his hand on the wet glass, he examined his face for the first time. Four deep gashes extended from his hairline to his jaw on the left side of his face. Nick knew he had been scarred for life. He saw Tommy looking up at him from the reflection in the mirror.

"Nick, you saved my life tonight. I didn't believe you about the tracks. I'm sorry."

"There was no way for you to have known that we were hunting a potential alien lifeform, Tommy. Even if Dale had told us the truth, we wouldn't have believed him. I feel sorry for the old man. And how in the world did that thing not kill him? I guess it doesn't matter now. Dead men tell no tales."

"Not quite," Tommy said scrubbing mud off his back with a luffa.

"What?" Nick turned around trying to interpret his friend's quizzical comment. "You didn't kill him, did you?"

"I left him up there chained right where you left him. I figured starving to death was worse than a bullet to the brain." Tommy grinned.

"But I heard shots."

"Yeah, I aimed the bullets as close to his head as I could. The bastard's probably deaf."

"We gotta go back up there, man. We have to know what he knows. There's a friggin' alien lizard in your front yard. My bulldog almost died trying to kill it! I want to know what that thing is!" Nick stated angrily. He couldn't believe Tommy hadn't shared the fact that Dale was still alive earlier. Nick felt like his best friend had been in denial ever since he had told him about the unusual footprints.

"Nick, look at me. If you wanna go up there, fine, but I can't go with you. I can't even walk, man. Besides, just like you said, we were lucky tonight. I seriously underestimated that thing. I'm down for just gettin' as far away from these mountains as we can."

"I know, I know. But I'm going back up there. We can take off afterward. Hurry up with your bath 'cuz I'm leaving as soon as you're done in here."

"What if there are more of those creatures in that mine? What are you gonna do?" Tommy asked genuinely concerned for Nick's life.

"How many grenades do you have downstairs?" Nick asked with a straight face. Tommy just smiled enlivened by Nick's bravado. "A bunch. But please be careful. You're my ride, man. I can't exactly drive. Just go in and out as fast as you can."

"I'm going to the kitchen to wash my face. Holler when you're ready to get out." Nick left the bathroom and went out to the backyard underneath the eaves and bathed Arnold with a medicated shampoo that he had bought from his vet for eighty dollars. The soap settled into the cuts in the dog's neck and chest causing Arnold to cry in discomfort. The dog would need stitches, but Nick wasn't about to do it himself. No, the bulldog's wounds would have to be treated by whomever Nick could find to help Tommy.

Nick was gingerly drying off Arnold when Tommy called him back into the bathroom. He took Arnold inside and searched for a clean t-shirt to put on him to keep his wounds from getting infected. The ornery bulldog bucked and chomped at each one Nick tried on him. Finally, Arnold chose a t-shirt he liked. It was a loose, faded Superman shirt, the kind you buy at the swap meet for a dollar. Nick reasoned that it must have felt good against Arnold's fur. The dog was downright happy to have it on. Arnold went to lay down in his bed and went to sleep without a care in the world.

Nick helped Tommy dry off and get dressed then went down into the cellar and got geared up in full tactical armor. He took with him a flashbang, a smoker, two concussion grenades, six clips, two handguns, a shotgun, and an MK18 stocked with heavy rounds. Nick was living in the Wild West now and he wasn't about to get blindsided by another lizard. And if he did get mortally wounded he would take the lizards to hell with him. Nick ran back upstairs and handed Tommy a shortwave radio.

"You look like you're about to invade the Hague. Haha." Tommy joked in awe of his friend's intimidating appearance, "I see you found my new optics."

"This is the lightest set I've ever used."

"Israeli military issue. They look good on you."

"Don't lie. They make me look like somebody's lab partner." Nick laughed, "I don't care. They work great. I'll be on channel five. If I'm not back in an hour you'll know you're next on the menu." Nick said handing Tommy his beloved AK49 and a single grenade. Tommy nodded in approval.

"Very comforting. Thanks." Tommy replied as he wound a roll of duct tape around both his ankles and thighs as a precautionary measure. Just because he couldn't feel his legs didn't mean he couldn't damage them and Tommy had every intention of using them again.

Nick went out to the garage and grabbed the sharpest ax he could find. He then walked over to the lizardman's body and hacked off its right forearm. He put the severed limb in a garbage bag and then taped the bag around his waist. Nick jumped into Tommy's Bronco and peeled off down the fire road fueled by a biting, slightly unnerving curiosity.

Nick approached the mine with his headlights off parking just shy of its entrance. He had backed the Bronco up facing downhill leaving the keys in the ignition in case he needed to make a quick getaway. The ex-soldier breached the mine with stealth and speed after activating his night optics. He could see everything inside the shaft as if it were midday. Nick ferreted through the underground caves committing every turn to memory. Ever since he was a kid Nick could memorize the route to a place he had just been. It was a skill that served him well as a C-COM operator. He made short work of navigating the cave system and cleared chamber after chamber with a ready trigger finger when an idea struck him. He realized he had been hastily exploring the interior of the mine without checking for the lizard's footprints. He cursed himself for making such a boneheaded mistake. Nick continued on carefully searching the ground for evidence of the lizardman's passage. After entering a narrow tunnel that headed south and east, he was able to make out the clawed marks of the lizardman's feet. He dutifully followed them not knowing where they might lead. He corked a concussion grenade and held it in the same hand as he held the stock of his assault rifle. Nick's focus was razor sharp as he delved deeper and deeper into no man's land.

Nick noticed that the further he went the larger the tunnel became. Eventually, the passageway took on enormous proportions before dead-ending at a giant corroded metal hatch whose giant wheeled crank was the diameter of a hula hoop. The creature's tracks led straight inside. Nick's heartbeat began to pound like a drum as he observed the door's stalwart construction. He took a deep breath, shouldered his rifle with the grenade still in his hand, and grabbed the crank to open the door. Searing heat singed Nick's fingers through his Teflon gants forcing him to withdraw his hands in pain. The door was scalding hot. An interesting security feature, Nick noted. Frustrated, he looked around for something that could pry the crank open but could find nothing. He thought about using both of his concussion grenades but knew better. Their combined explosions would barely dent the massive metal works. Whatever was behind that door would remain a mystery to him, for now. He took mental notes of the door's design in case he was ever crazy enough to come back. 'Screw it, he thought and turned around.

It took him another fifteen minutes to retrace his steps and clear the rest of the mine. He was confident that he and Dale were alone. Nick returned to the caved-in tunnel and shimmied through the opening which was even tighter than before because of Nick's gear. When he made it to the other side he saw Dale sitting up against the wall bathed in the eerie red light of his battery-powered citronella lantern. When Dale saw him, he didn't recognize Nick. He hobbled up to stand on his one good leg and sported an outright hospitable smile.

"Hey, alright. Am I happy to see you fellers? Those two hunters in that lodge down there shot me up pretty good. Left me for dead in here. You're here to take me to the city, right?" Dale said, his eyes begging for mercy. Nick stayed quiet. He wanted to know whom Dale thought he was talking to. "Hey, now look partner. I held up my end of the bargain. I've been feeding him real good just like you wanted. I mean I've been taking real good care of him. Now, how's about a little TLC for me, huh?" Dale implored. Nick beat Dale's face with the butt of his rifle knocking a few of the old man's teeth out. Dale whimpered in pain donning a look of complete servility.

"Where's the creature?" Nick questioned in as different and ominous a voice as possible.

"I don't know. I've been chained up." Dale tugged at the very bonds Nick had placed around his neck. "If ya let me loose...I can grab the monitor and check for ya." Dale promised.

"Hurry up," Nick commanded shooting the chain from around Dale's neck. The dirty old man limped off into the darkness and came back with a touchscreen tablet. Nick couldn't believe his eyes. The internet had been down since the collection centers had closed. And here this hermit was using an electronic device that was able to uplink to a satellite connection.

"Okay. Okay. Just give me one second. Okay, here it is, see. Wait! Ah, just wait. I dunno what's wrong with this thing." Dale stuttered looking desperately around the inside of the chamber. "I don't understand."

"What don't you understand?" Nick yelled threatening his rifle butt again. Dale cowered and held the tablet up to Nick's masked face.

"Ya see, it says he's in here with us, right now." Dale slowly turned his head back toward Nick.

Nick looked at the black monitor. He was baffled. Dale, a homeless drifter had been monitoring an alien predator. Nick grew tired of the charade and took off his helmet and goggles revealing his identity. Dale fell on his ass in shock. The old man had played his cards for all to see. Nick whipped out the bag containing the lizardman's severed arm and threw it against Dale's chest. Dale looked down at his lap where the proof of the creature's death fell and gasped in horror. He turned his torso toward the cave wall and began weeping silently.

"What have you done? Why? Is it dead? Oh no. Oh no!" Dale cried. He picked up the severed arm from the ground turning it over wrist-side up apparently looking for something. "Oh no. Nooo."

"What is this thing, Dale? You might as well tell me what you know." Nick probed putting pressure on the old man's still festering bullet wounds.

"Damn, you guys. Damn you to hell, both of you. You screwed me. Everything's screwed now." Dale sobbed frantically his eyes filled with horror. "They'll never let me in now. They're never gonna let me in."

"Dale, dammit tell me what is going on? What is behind that big ass door down there?" Nick asked pointing in the direction he believed the hatch was located. Dale wouldn't talk. He just sat there mumbling incoherently.

Nick suddenly got the idea to try a different approach. He remembered the military interrogations he had taken part in back when had served in Iraq. Whenever the interrogators got stonewalled due to their use of over-aggressive methods they employed an opposing technique to elicit information from informants, gratification. Nick holstered his handgun and knelt beside Dale who was a little surprised at the new posture.

"Hey, man I'm impressed by your ability to live in here with that thing. Seriously." Nick whispered to the shivering, broken man. "I mean, why didn't it kill you? Tell me, Dale, why are you still alive? After you tell me, I'll take you home with me. I'll clean you up and you'll get to live in that cabin all by yourself. Me and my friend are just gonna give it to you. All you have to do is tell me what the creature is and why it didn't kill you."

Dale looked up at Nick earnestly. He held up his wrist. Underneath Dale's pale skin, a dim glowing diode pulsed.

"As long as you've got one of these in ya the lizards won't hurt you. But it don't matter now. I'm a goner. They're gonna kill me for sure. I tried to warn ya. Ya know I did."

"Who is they, Dale?" Nick stroked the old man's face as if he were a child. "What are these creatures? For the love of God, tell me something. Who left you in charge of monitoring that thing? What's behind the door, Dale? Come on!"

"Three months ago, some men came in here and told me what was gonna happen. They were dressed up just like you. They told me they needed my he..." Dale's explanation was interrupted by a signal that came from the monitoring tablet. Nick picked it up and looked at it. A flashing beacon hovered over their exact location. Within seconds Dale started foaming at the mouth before coughing up tons of blood. Nick observed the diode on the underside of the man's wrist. It was pulsating faster and faster and emitted a pink glow. Dale gasped for air clearly on the verge of death.

"Tell me what you know, dammit. Please!" Nick beseeched the dying man holding him in his arms.

Dale, staring at the ceiling of the mine, slurred a final sentence through blood-covered lips.

"They...have always...been...here." The light in Dale's wrist went dark. Nick looked back at the monitor. Its screen suddenly locked and then began to heat up tremendously. Nick dropped the device to the ground as it smoldered and fizzled. Bright sparks jetted outward from behind the device's screen. Nick couldn't understand what was happening. He double-timed it out of the mine. He wanted to put as much distance between himself and Dale's dead body as he could. Nick had a strong feeling that someone had been monitoring the old man, and whoever it was, had killed him to keep him from talking. If that were indeed the case, then the people responsible were probably already on their way to investigate the scene. Nick drove back to the cabin eager to share his experience with Tommy. What had Dale meant by his last words? Who was it that had promised the old man and what carrot were they dangling in front of him to get him to do their bidding? Nick had a million burning questions and no way to answer them. His thoughts returned to the massive door he could not open. Its image seared into Nick's memory. He would return one day and crank that sucker open. He could only imagine the possibilities of what existed on the other side.

Chapter 5: The Shelters

Leila felt completely vulnerable. Consumed with fear, she hadn't come out of the corner of the shelter since waking from her drugged stupor hours ago. The reality of where she was had already begun to settle in. The young girl could only look around in horror hoping someone, anyone, would reunite her with her parents. The shelter was gigantic and looked and felt like the hold of an enormous cargo ship. Its looming red walls were rough to the touch and dingy. There was a hole, the size of a jacuzzi, in the middle of the floor that people were defecating into. The smell of the place was stultifying forcing Leila to breathe through her mouth. The sounds were even worse. She had to put her hands over her ears to block out the continuous moaning, crying, and screaming. The shelter was a living hell and there seemed to be no escape.

Leila had no idea where her parents were and dared not call out for them. She wanted to remain invisible. The memory of the creature's piercing yellow eyes continued to play games with her mind. The young girl kept scanning the interior of the shelter making sure the monster wasn't lurking around in some dark corner. Seeing that Leila had come to, a woman, whose medical gown was brown with dirt, gently walked over to her. She knelt down beside the ten year-old and kindly introduced herself.

"Hello, child. I'm Marsala. I know you must be afraid. We all are. It's okay to be scared. They've separated all of us. None of us know where our families are." Marsala shared. "What's your name?"

"Leila." The young girl struggled to form the words.

"Okay, Leila. I am a friend. I promise I won't hurt you, okay?"

"You mean, my mother and father...there not here?" Leila began to cry.

"I'm sorry, Leila." Marsala held Leila. "But no. Your parents are probably in another shelter somewhere."

"But why? They told us we would be together!" Leila sobbed her mouth remaining agape as sadness poured out from her spirit.

"No one knows why? I have been here since they opened the shelters. Do you remember the date today?"

Leila sobered up at the thought of such an objective question, "Today is...today is the 28th of August."

"Good job, Leila. That means I have been down here for thirty-three days and counting." Marsala, with as much empathy as a human can have for another person, held Leila at arm's length and said, "I have to tell you some things about this place that

you have to know if you want to stay safe, okay?"
Leila simply nodded her head.

"Do you see those men in the corner over there?
Don't look at them too long. Stay away from them.
They are bad men. They will try to hurt you and
take your food. That hole, over there, in the middle
of the floor is the only toilet but that doesn't stop
people from going to the bathroom on the floor. So,
it is important that you never touch the floor with
your hands, okay."

"Okay." Leila agreed on the verge of crying
again.

"Every so often we are fed food in little silver
pouches. But I want to talk to you about who
delivers the food, or, I should say, what delivers the
food. Do you see the hatch over there next to that
really big lady with the orange hair?"

"Yes."

"It's scalding hot to the touch. If you touch it, it
will burn the skin off your hands. So don't ever try

to open it. But when that door does open you are going to see monsters come through it."

At this Leila brightened throwing Marsaleh completely off balance. The thought of a grownup believing, verifying what she, herself, had seen brought her out of her shell a little. That is before she remembered how awful they looked.

"I know about the monsters. I saw one outside. I tried telling my mom and dad but they didn't believe me." Leila's breath became shortened causing her to hiccup as she spoke.

"You saw one up there? How?" Marsala asked.

"I wasn't supposed to see it. They tried to hide it but when it came out of the helicopter it turned and saw me. It was so scary."

"Don't worry, Leila. All they do is come in and drop off the food. But you cannot look at them. If you so much as look in their direction they might hurt you. I have seen them kill three people already. And in here, when you die, they drop you into that hole."

There seemed to be no end to the bad news. Leila couldn't even think straight. The idea of seeing the monsters again terrified her. She took a little comfort in the fact that she wouldn't be singled out. It would be easy for her to hide among the others.

Marsala continued, "We are given water more than we are fed. There are tiny holes in the walls. See them? They are about the size of oranges. Well, when the water comes everyone fights to drink it. You must get water, Leila. You must find a way. This is why I've come over here. I want to help you. Just before the water comes out of those holes you will feel a rumble in the walls. As soon as you feel this rumble, go to the holes. You will be the first to drink. Be quick about it though, don't take too much time or you will be trampled by others who are bigger and stronger than you. Do you understand?" Marsala got up to leave but Leila grabbed the frayed edges of her gown.

"Please don't leave me. Please."

"Listen, Leila. You must be strong now. I have two little girls somewhere inside the shelters and I pray someone is helping them like I'm helping you. But you have to learn how to survive right now or else you could die in here. I'm sorry, Leila. I'll come around when I can to check on you, but you must learn how to be on your own." Marsala got up and left the young girl crying into the lap of her gown. Stricken with grief, the young girl accidentally put her palms on the ground and immediately recoiled them in fear.

The longest Leila had ever been separated from her parents had been earlier that summer. Coffee had enrolled her daughter in an outdoor activity camp where the children hiked to the top of Table Mountain spending three nights and four days underneath the stars of the African sky. By the third day, Leila was more than ready to go home. The thought of being disconnected from her parents for an extended period broke the little girl's heart. She just sat alone for some time by herself. There was no way for her to tell how long because there were no clocks or windows inside the shelter. Leila was content with staying put where she was, forever, that is, until she felt the rumble in the walls.

Leila put her tiny ear up against the shelter's bulwarks. Just as Marsaleh had described, she could hear water rushing toward her. She looked around for the closest hole in the wall. It was three meters away and to her left. There was no one by it. She somehow managed the strength to quietly walk over to it, more out of curiosity than thirst. A small rivulet of clear water streamed out of all the holes at the same time. Leila did just as Marsaleh instructed and was able to get two mouthfuls before being pushed aside by three older girls. Leila returned to her small little corner of hell and watched as many of the inhabitants of the shelter descended into violence and chaos. Men beat each other, women pulled each other's hair, and the old and the young were forgotten as everyone vied for survival. Witnessing people behave in such a manner crippled Leila's understanding of the world, of society. Some of the inhabitants, who had not quenched their thirst for some time, appeared as though they were at death's door. Two older men, after not getting to drink, solemnly walked to the middle of the room and volunteered themselves into the hole. No one paid them any mind. They were too busy satisfying their own desires. Leila didn't understand why more people hadn't paid attention to the rumble. She wondered where the hole in the middle of the room led to. She thought that maybe the hole could be used to escape but then imagined a giant incinerator at its bottom.

Marsala, eventually, made it back over to Leila and smiled, "I saw you drink. Good job. Remember to do that every time and you'll be fine. I gotta go." Just as quickly as she came Marsaleh left again. Leila decided to observe the older woman who had so graciously helped her. She was taller and much slimmer than her mother with bronze skin and brown hair just like her. Leila couldn't tell her nationality by simply looking at her, but judging by Marsaleh's accent, Leila thought she might be from the West Indies or maybe Trinidad. Marsala walked around the shelter talking to many different people as she went. She wasn't chatting but discussing something that seemed very important, but there was no telling what. Marsala finally walked over to one of the men in the corner, the same corner she had told Leila to stay away from. She and a tall, brutish-looking fellow disappeared behind a wall of other large men. Leila was instinctively curious about this and for the first time since arriving inside the veritable prison, she began to walk around trying to sneak peeks at the men in the corner without being seen.

"Hey, you!" an older boy barked out of nowhere. Leila didn't acknowledge the boy even though she thought he seemed nice enough to talk to. "You're the new girl. Don't worry, you won't be for long. People always come tumbling down here. My name's Jacob. I'm twelve. How old are you?"

"Why are you talking to me?" Leila asked her hazel eyes flaring at the young boy. "Why don't you just leave me alone?"

"You need friends in here. You'll see. You won't be able to get food or water if you don't find people that will help you." Jacob answered unphased by Leila's apprehensive personality.

"Why should I trust you? What do you want?"

"I know a secret way to always get food."

"Great, but why are you telling me? What do you want from me?" Leila fired back turning her head and walking away from Jacob hoping he would not follow her, but he did.

"I dunno. I just thought you looked normal is all. People in here can get kinda crazy sometimes. And those big guys over there are always trying to make sure that us little guys stay weak, and don't eat. We gotta stick together, you, me, and all the other kids in here. We're all just like you. None of us know where our parents are either."

Leila's heart opened a smidge and she turned around and eyed Jacob up and down. His gown was much dirtier than Marsaleh's and she had been inside the shelters for over a month. Jacob reminded her of a boy she used to know at her school who, for some reason, always wanted to talk with her. She hadn't understood why just as she didn't understand now, but she eventually came to enjoy the boy's company. She thought that Jacob might be the same kind of boy.

"Okay, what's your secret? Tell me and we can be friends." She grabbed Jacob's hand and led him over to her dark little corner. The two sat down together and Jacob began to explain his secret.

"When the ogres bring the food in," Jacob explained, "Wait, oh, I forgot there's ogres in here. Don't look at 'em or they'll kill you."

"I know I've already seen one."

"You've already seen one? But you just got here." Jacob pointed out. "How?"

"I saw one up there. I wasn't supposed to, but I did." Leila answered pointing to the surface.

"Wait, you saw an ogre before you came down here and you still came?" Jacob asked astounded. He couldn't understand why anyone would do such a thing knowingly. "What are you crazy? Anyway, when the ogres bring the food in it'll be piled real high on a stretcher. You know, the kind of thing they use in football matches when the players get hurt." Leila nodded her head. She and her father used to watch football matches together all the time. "Well, the ogres always drop some on their way in. And everyone is too afraid to go near them to grab 'em, especially the big guys. I always grab 'em real quick and most of the time the ogres never even see me. You gotta eat what's inside the packages fast or somebody might try to punch you and swipe it out of your hands."

"That sounds so scary," Leila confessed imagining the feat in her head.

"It is, but it's also kind of fun. And the thing of it is, I haven't missed a meal yet." Jacob bragged petting his stomach proudly. "Look around. Some of these people haven't eaten anything in weeks. And some other people in here will bash you to make sure they stay fed." Leila looked around and could see what Jacob had rightly pointed out. Many people were starving, their faces gaunt, their bodies too lean. Hunger had sunken their eyes into their sockets and caused them to move about very slowly as if in a trance of some kind.

"I'm Leila." She whispered not wanting anyone else to hear her name. For some reason, she feared telling Jacob even though she liked him. It was as though telling someone her name was the same thing as walking around naked for everyone to see, to judge. "This place is so awful. Why is this happening? Who would do this to us?"

"It's probably the ogres. Some people say they are aliens from another planet. But to me, to me..." Jacob leaned in near Leila's ear to finish his thoughts, "They look like dinosaurs. Like if you took a dinosaur and a person and put 'em in a blender. I think they're cool-looking. I mean, you wouldn't want to be locked in a room with one of them, but I bet you they can do some amazing stuff like jump super high and run really, really fast."

"I think they're terrifying," Leila added. "They look like the Devil."

The two shared a long moment of silence before Jacob stood up. "Well, when that door opens you'll hear a squeal that sounds like a mouse getting squished under a boot. It'll be followed by two loud clicks. That's the signal to run over to the door. Don't forget, okay. I'll see you later, Leila. It was nice meeting you."

"Bye, Jacob." Leila watched Jacob leave just as she did Marsala. He went over to some of the other kids in the shelter, mostly boys, and pointed her out to them. She was hoping Jacob was telling them how cool she was. They looked at her from across the room but didn't come over even though she kind of wanted them to. Leila was getting sleepy but didn't feel safe closing her eyelids. She feared where she might wake up next. The young girl fought the urge to sleep for some time but eventually dozed off sitting upright with her knees to her chest.

Leila dreamed of the monster. He had trapped her parents in a dungeon and was laughing and growling at them. Her mother screamed for Leila's help but there was nothing she could do but watch as her parents were tortured by the disgusting creature and its evil henchmen. Their cackles and grunts filled her inner dreamscape with turmoil and hopelessness. But during her dream, a warm light grew from a small pin-sized glow until it encompassed everything she could see. The light vibrated and hummed with a presence of beingness, as though it had a personality. The light began speaking to her in a low, oscillating voice, "Do not be afraid, Leila. This nightmare will soon end. You will be freed from this place. I have prepared a way for you. I am with you now. Do not be afraid..." Leila called out to the voice wanting to know who it was, but it had nothing more to say. The light imploded inward into the size of a small glowing orb that began to flitter up to her face like a moth around a flame. Then it settled into her outstretched hands before disappearing altogether. Suddenly, Leila found herself back in the dungeon where her parents were suffering at the hands of the cruel monsters. But instead of being afraid, Leila found the courage to push the monsters out of the way and when she did they turned into cute cartoon baby lizards. She then freed her mom and dad from bondage. The three of them were reunited in love and peace. A newfound power blossomed inside Leila's spirit that broke through the darkness of the nightmare. Leila, shining brightly like an angel, threw open the gates of the dungeon with the might of a titan, and as they opened a high-pitched squeal sounded off. It was so loud it woke Leila up.

Leila quickly realized that the squeal in her dream had come from the hatch that was being wrenched open from outside of the shelter. The squeal was followed by two loud knocks. Leila ran to where a bunch of the other children had gathered on one side of the entrance. She was still half-asleep. Everything that was happening to her unfolded in slow motion. Her body was teeming with the redemptive energies of the dream state she had just snapped out of.

"Get ready," a boy said in Leila's general direction possibly to the children standing to the left of her. The hatch flung open banging on the interior wall with a thunderous clang. A roar more powerful than a lion rang out into the shelter. Terrified screams and the sounds of bare feet scurrying into the darkest parts of the cell followed. Three large monsters stepped through the opening carrying a large litter teeming with silver packets of food. The creatures were as tall as basketball players and covered in brightly colored scales that were distinct to each one. In the light of the shelter, they seemed not nearly as fearsome as the hooded monster she had seen above ground. Just as Jacob had described, many of the food packets slid off of the pile and onto the grime-covered floor prompting dozens of children to swoop in behind the monsters and grab them. But Leila noticed something very curious. The beasts who brought the food seemed to purposefully mishandle the litter. It was as clear as day to her, but no one else seemed to pick up on it. Something inside her told her that the lizardmen were loosening the food packets on purpose for the children. The implications of this subtle understanding exploded inside Leila's mind. The great wall of fear that the creatures' physical presence emanated lessened for her dramatically. Maybe it was the voice in her dream, she thought. But whatever the reason, she no longer felt afraid of the monsters even though they appeared extremely aggressive.

Leila, to the shock of everyone in the shelter, walked up to the litter while the beasts were setting it down and took two food packets off the top. Gasps could be heard throughout the chamber and a strange moment of silence ensued as the two lizardmen carrying the food looked at one another, perplexed by the young girl's audacity. The lizardman, farthest from her, pushed aside his comrade and snarled into Leila's face. Leila, inexplicably stood there shaking not out of terror but out of respect for the awesome strength of the being standing in front of her. In a move just absurd as the one she had just made, Leila lifted one of her food packets to the menacing creature suggesting that he take it for himself. The lizardman tilted his head to the side like a bird trying to figure out a feeder and grinned a grin that only Leila could see. Then his eyes narrowed. Realizing the little girl had just made a show of their unprecedented interaction, the guard snatched the food packet from Leila's tiny hand. He stood up slowly lifting the packet up into the air so everyone could see it and emptied its contents onto the floor. He then tossed the empty packet into the hole in the middle of the room with amazing accuracy. Leila instantly felt responsible for denying someone a possible meal. But the creature wasn't done. He looked at his fellow guard and made three clicking noises from the back of his throat. They both growled fiercely looking around the room daring for anyone to approach them as the girl had done. The lizardman in charge, while looking Leila straight in the eyes, ordered his comrade to pick up a gigantic armful of food packets and drop them down the hole in the floor. Leila's heart followed the foodstuffs into the blackness. She could feel the flood of hatred from everyone else in the chamber envelope her like a cloud of toxic gas. The reptilians then started to exit the cell. The guard who first approached Leila faced her again letting

157

off a slight chuckle before shutting the door onto her miserable fate. As soon as the hatch shut and the wheel locked, a man yelled, "Kill her!" at the top of his lungs.

"Throw her in the damn hole with our food!" another woman screeched. People began to swarm Leila, encircling her, and spitting venomous words in her direction. But before they could push, punch, and pummel her all the children in the shelters, Jacob at the helm, gathered around the young girl. Seeing the children together, in one place, staring back at them brought the mob to a halt. No one was going to cast the first stone by breaking a child's face. Instead, they turned and began fighting over what rations remained.

The children rushed Leila away from the fray and began peppering her with questions about her unbelievable encounter with the lizardmen. Jacob pushed the other children aside smiling.

"You are crazy! I thought you were gonna piss yourself when you saw them. Instead, you actually walked up to one! Wow. I didn't know you had it in you. Everybody is talking about what you did." Leila blushed shyly as she was introduced to her peers. The children were in complete awe of her. Not only had Leila shown more moxy than anyone in the history of the shelter's short existence, but she had also managed to unite a rather unseemly, insignificant portion of the shelter's inhabitants, the children. Leila would need them for she had just painted a target on her back. Her actions had robbed the food that would have otherwise fed dozens of hungry people who now glared at her through darkened eyes bulging with contempt.

Chapter 6: On the Road Again

Nick, Arnold, and Tommy had put a lot of miles in between them and the cabin. Before leaving, the two men stuffed the lizardman's headless body into one of the meat lockers in the cabin's cellar in case they ever needed more proof. Tommy, true to his word, had preserved the creature's head in a jar hiding it in a blue cooler that they had put in the back of Nick's truck. They were headed back to San Diego to try their hand at fishing. The friends had agreed on taking Nick's truck as it could carry more of Tommy's belongings which included a four-person fishing boat now hitched to the back. They were chin deep in a conversation concerning the implications of Nick's experience with Dale.

"I just don't understand why the government would entrust an old hermit living in a mine shaft with such a huge responsibility?" Nick argued.

"You said it yourself, Nick, nobody would believe him if he talked. Before you saw that lizard, Dale could have told you everything he knew about the dang thing and you would've just laughed your ass off." Tommy stated.

"Oh, and I suppose you wouldn't?"

"I would at least think about it afterward."

"Well, it doesn't matter at all what Dale did or didn't know. It's about what's behind that door." Nick dreamed of it, its size, its materiality. "You should have seen it, Tommy. It was huge."

"Yeah, yeah, yeah. You keep talking about that damn door." Tommy pointed out. "I don't know why a door is more significant to you compared to all the other bombs the old man dropped on us."

"Because, if you would have seen it you would have felt it. It was a portal to another world. Imagine what's on the other side."

"More lizards for one. Not to mention the likelihood of noxious gases that far down underground. You're acting like there's a magical candy land down there filled with horny virgins or somethin'."

"You just love doing that don't you?"

"Doing what? Expressing rationality."

"No, every time I mention something about the mine you naysay it like a Doubting Thomas or something."

"C'mon, Nick. Ever since you got back from interrogating Dale it's like you've been floatin' on cloud nine. But that's not what troubles me. Ya see, I don't think you're allowing yourself to accept all the screwed up things that we have been allowed to believe our entire lives. Not to mention what the lizards mean in relation to the collection."

"And I don't think you're allowing yourself to fully experience the scope of the world in which we now live. A world where two sentient species are sharing the same planet. Those were Dale's last words, Tommy, 'They've always been here!'"

Tommy repeated Dale's now iconic last words at the same time as Nick to further illustrate his point that his compadre was being all too naive about the whole thing. Tommy knew that there was a connection between the creature they had killed and the collection. He just couldn't see what exactly it was. He felt as though he needed one more piece of the puzzle to figure things out for himself. After, spending a couple of miles consumed in their own thoughts, their attentions became focused on a plume of thick smoke rising ahead on the lonely highway. Not knowing what to expect Tommy put his left hand on the shotgun in between the two front seats.

"What do we have here?" Nick asked driving up on a rag-tag bunch stranded by their broken-down van on the side of the road.

"Look at those poor bastards," Tommy said without much empathy.

"I'm gonna pull over." Nick declared in a tone that conveyed to Tommy that arguing over the matter wasn't worth the hassle.

"Alright, whatever. Do your worst. You don't know squat about Dodge's anyway." Tommy ribbed. Nick just shook his head before pushing in the parking brake with his foot. He got out and walked over to one of the guys who was trying like the dickens not to burn his hands on an overheated engine. Arnold jumped from Tommy's lap and pushed his bullnose against the partially rolled down driver's side window.

"You guys look like you need some help," Nick stated. Instead of the warm welcome, he thought he would receive, the people shied away from him eventually hopping back inside the van and locking the doors. Nick approached the front end of the van and glanced at his reflection in the driver's side window. The scar on his face was still fresh enough to ooze puss and was, no doubt, the reason all but one of the strangers ran for cover. Nick looked every bit the part of a serial killer. A skinny man with a pink shirt and faded blue ball cap pulled his head out from under the hood of the van and regarded Nick cautiously.

"You and me both." The man said brandishing a wrench, a clear sign that he would use it to smash Nick's head in if he had to. He could try, Nick thought to himself.

"You should see the bear." Nick lied deflecting the man's reservations. They both shared a quick laugh relieving some of the tension from the situation.

"Are you a mechanic?" The man asked before correcting himself, "I mean, were you a mechanic?" In that sentence alone Nick measured a great deal about the man, that and the fact that he hadn't registered for the shelters.

"No, but I know my way around an engine or two," Nick answered casually. "What happened?"

"Well, the darn thing just started puttering about ten miles back. It kept making a whirling noise and then there was a loud snap. Five miles later the temperature gauge started going bonkers. I pulled over here and smoke just started billowing out of the engine."

"Can I take a look?" Nick asked.

"Be my guest. I would definitely appreciate it. I'd rather not be out here in the dark with my family, if you get my drift. I mean, if you're what the good guys look like around here I'd hate to see the bad guys."

Nick could only laugh but the words hurt his feelings. He still hadn't adjusted to his new grizzly appearance. But just as Tommy would have to learn how to deal with not being able to use his legs, as temporary as he hoped it would be, so would Nick have to cope with his disfigurement.

Nick stuck his head into the engine compartment and nosed around. The timing belt had snapped and a piece of it had lodged itself inside the vent of the radiator, stopping the fan from rotating. It was a simple enough fix but Nick didn't have a spare belt and they were still pretty far from anything resembling a service station.

"Well, my friend, I've got good news and bad news. Which do you want first?" Nick asked stretching his arms out against the lip of the van's grill.

"Just give it to me." The man said clapping his hands against his thighs, "Straight as an arrow."

Nick obliged, "Easy to fix if you only had the parts. The nearest place we could go salvaging is still another twenty miles south from here. You're kind of up a creek."

"We've got paddles, though." The man insisted pointing to the bikes on the roof of the van. He didn't want to appear too eager for the kindness of strangers.

"Where are you headed?" Nick asked trying to be polite. The man took a step back regarding the situation in a new light.

"South." He answered. Nick chuckled aware of the reason behind the man's reticence to fork over any information about their destination. Nick knew that there was no way the guy could fix the belt on his own, the repair required a torque wrench with an elbow, a tool not too many people had just lying around. Nick had one, but he wasn't about to fork it over and he sure as hell wasn't going to make the long trek to get the parts and then double back to install them for the guy, even though that would have been the nicest thing to do. But these weren't the nicest times. It would be reckless of Nick, especially with Tommy and Arnold needing medical attention, to burn through a quarter tank of gas on behalf of anyone so far from their ultimate destination. Nick looked back to the truck judging its capacity. He then looked over at the boat hitched to the back and sprouted an idea.

"Hold on for just a minute, will ya?" Nick asked before walking back over to his truck so that he and Tommy could have a word.

"What's the matter with the van?" Tommy wanted to know.

"Timing belt snapped. Bits of it got lodged in the radiator which caused the engine to overheat." Nick stated. "Whaddya say we throw the lot of 'em in the boat and take 'em wherever they need to go? If the van is important we can stow it off the road back there and they can come back for it later."

"Fine." Tommy looked off down the road. "Let's get a move on while we still got light."

Nick walked back to the man with the ball cap who had already closed the hood of the van. He was standing with his hands on his hips still holding onto the crescent wrench.

"I've got an idea." Nick began, "You don't have the tools and I don't have the time to help you. But, if you want, you and your family can pile into our fishing boat. I still have a little room in the truck bed for more stuff, but you'd have to be frugal with what you bring. I'm headed to Imperial Beach in San Diego. I'd be more than happy to let you out somewhere along the way."

"San Diego?" the man's eyes brightened. "Wait just a second."

Nick stood in the middle of the road as the man in the ball cap consorted with his rather large family. After a moment, they began to trickle out of the van one by one taking a bag or two each with them. The man returned to Nick. His body language sang a much different tune than the defensive postures he had been exhibiting.

"Robert Hansen." He said shaking Nick's hand. "This is my family." Robert went down the line introducing each multi-colored child and his plain Jane wife to Nick. "We'd absolutely appreciate a lift. We're going to Spring Valley. You know it?"

"Of course. Nice to meet all of you. I'm Nick and that's Tommy and my bulldog, Arnold, inside." Arnold let out a single bark wanting nothing more than to say hello to all the new smells and friends. "We are coming back from a pretty dangerous hunting trip. We've decided to fish the coast for our suppers from now on. You're more than welcome to cruise with us, okay?"

Nick's introduction worked like a charm. The family, anxious to be on the road again, packed their belongings into the back of Nick's truck before climbing into the boat.

"Are you gonna just leave your van on the side of the road?" Nick asked Robert. His pear-shaped wife closed in on the conversation.

"No, I don't think that's a good idea, Robert. We should definitely hide it somewhere. Maybe, Clarissa knows someone who can come back and fix it." Robert's wife, Amanda, butted in.

"Yeah, let's roll it off the road." Robert agreed.

"Alright, there's a turnoff back there. Amanda if you steer, Robert and I can push you over there behind those trees." Nick suggested.

"Okay, great. Thank you so much. You're so kind." Amanda added getting behind the wheel. Nick and Robert pushed the van in place working up a good sweat in the process. When they were done Nick told Robert to ride with them in the cab so that he could tell them where to go. Much to Nick's initial dismay, Robert insisted that his wife sit inside the truck. When she hopped inside the extra cab Arnold bounded onto her lap to greet her. Amanda laughed letting the big dog lick her all over.

"Oh, I just love bulldogs. I had one growing up. His name was Sam, short for Samson. And, oh, was he a lively son of a gun. He used to pee on my mattress whenever I wouldn't let him sleep with me."

"Yep, sounds like a bully, alright," Tommy confirmed shaking Amanda's hand. "Don't pet him too hard. The poor thing got wounded by a bear."

Predictably, Amanda couldn't help but start talking Nick and Tommy's ears off. And when she wasn't talking to them she was talking to Arnold who lapped up the attention greedily. But as they put up with her nonstop digging about the two men's domestic lives they couldn't help but hear her mention a doctor living in the place where the family was headed.

"A doctor?" Nick asked wanting to stop the truck in the middle of the road.

"Yes, Terrence is an excellent hip, knee, and foot surgeon. Or, I should say Terrence was an excellent surgeon. I doubt they have the facilities necessary for him to continue his practice with the same level of quality where we are going." Amanda answered her mousey bob bouncing along with the bumps in the road.

"What exactly is this place we are taking you to?" Tommy probed on the sly. He looked at Nick after he asked his question and then continued. "You can see that I'm in pretty bad shape. I'd like to use my legs again. Do you think this Terrence could help me?"

"I don't see why not. Once Robert tells Clarissa how you helped us I am sure she would be willing to at least let him give you a diagnosis."

"You're going to live in a church?" Nick questioned trying to form an image in his mind from the thousands of bits of information she had already shared with them.

"No. We are a part of a large church called Maranatha. Most of the branches were located in the southwest: California, Arizona, New Mexico, Colorado, and Nevada. Once the government announced its plan to initiate the mark of the beast our entire church began to develop a plan for living our lives completely independent from the government. So, we formed a camp, out in the open, in Jamul, very close to Spring Valley. It's been a huge success and we already have over two hundred and fifty members. God willing, we will grow into a powerful community of believers, living according to the teachings of Jesus Christ."

"Mark of the Beast?" Tommy asked laughing. Normally, Tommy would endlessly harass a woman like Amanda. But he sought to use the woman's convictions to prove to Nick the implications of what they now knew could and would change the world. "How interesting."

"Well just about everybody knows about the sign of the Devil. It says clearly in Revelations 13:16 that the mark of the beast will be placed inside the right hands of the wicked, so that they may trade, and subsist in Babylon." Amanda assured them. "Heck, the end of the world is now just about as popular a subject as sports or celebrity rehabs."

"You see, Nick. This is what I'm talking about." Tommy said. He leaned in a little after rolling down his window. He wanted the onrush of air to provide a bit of privacy from the Bible beater sitting in the back. "The stuff we stumbled upon is absolutely epic. It affects everything. This mark, the one she's talking about, you've seen it. You said Dale had one in his wrist, remember?"

Nick flashed Tommy a look of impatience. He had come too close to speaking openly about what they now knew. The two friends had already agreed not to tell anyone about their encounter with the lizardman until they knew more about what was going on. Besides, Nick wasn't ready to associate anything biblical with what had happened to them. He was much more interested in the prospect of living in a world where the existence of extraterrestrial beings was fact and not fiction.

Tommy got the hint and returned his seat to an upright position stemming the line of the conversation he desired to pursue. They drove much of the rest of the way in silence. Amanda told the men which exit to take off the interstate then closed her eyes for a while but secretly did not sleep. She wanted to eavesdrop on what the two men had been talking about but unfortunately uncovered nothing. Arnold, sensing no more attention could be gleaned from the woman returned to Tommy's lap and stuck his head out of the window letting the air pass through his flapping jowls.

Nick exited the interstate curving around the turnpike for the 94 east. The hills around eastern San Diego were surprisingly green for a late summer evening. The cataclysmic weather the scientist had foreseen was playing out to be a cruel joke. The sky still maintained its crimson complexion, and the air its intense humidity, but aside from those two factors along with the occasional thunderstorm, nothing even remotely calamitous had happened at all. Nick was frustrated by this. He secretly wanted to face a real storm for the first time in his life. They drove another twenty miles before stopping at a wooden cattle gate with a sign hanging from it. Its signage had been carved out by hand and painted turquoise. "Maranatha" it read, swaying to and fro in the gentle breeze. Having reached their destination, the Hansen clan began cheering from inside the boat. The sound roused Amanda from her fake sleep. She clearly wished to be surrounded by the joy the rest of her family was experiencing.

A man in a cowboy hat was sitting in a lawn chair on the other side of the gate, a clipboard and walkie-talkie in his hand. He took his sweet time standing up but when he did both Tommy and Nick couldn't believe how tall he was. The man swung his legs through the wooden fencing and approached Nick's truck cautiously.

"Howdy, there. Looks like you guys put in some hard miles. No worries. You're here now and that's all that matters. What's your reservation number?" the tall man asked peering from underneath the curved brim of his cowboy hat.

Before Nick could speak Amanda chimed in from the back seat, "394!" The man looked down at the list on his clipboard and radioed a code to someone on the other end. He just stood there waiting for the person to radio him back. Nick couldn't help but notice a large sidearm strapped to the cowboy's leather belt.

The code came back to the tall drink of water who leaned in onto Nick's door adopting a more casual demeanor. "Mrs. Hansen, I presume."

"That's right. That's my family in the boat back there." She assured the man.

"Well, it says here you've only got seven in your group. I count nine here if I'm not mistaken."

"Our van broke down just outside of Julian and these kind gentlemen were nice enough to drive us all the way here," Amanda added with a smile.

"Well, praise God for the both of ya." The tall man exclaimed looking the two men up and down without ever moving his head. "And what do we have here? Who's this fella?"

"That's Arnold. I'm Nick and that's Tommy. We're gonna be fishermen from now. We had a pretty rough go of it in the mountains." Nick explained.

"Oh, I see. Yeah, it can be rough country up there if ya let it. But fishing is a good honest trade and it'll keep your bellies full down here. More than hunting will. We don't have much game 'round these parts 'less you like coyote and rattlesnake meat. My name's Kai." The name struck Nick and Tommy as being odd for a cowboy. Kai sensed their bewilderment. "Yeah, I'm what happens when a cowboy marries a hippie. I love God and country and I don't like 'tie boys' or the boxes they're always trying to put people in."

"Haha, that's a good one," Tommy said genuinely amused. Nick could tell that Tommy liked the guy.

Kai stepped back from the vehicle so that he could address everyone in the caravan. "Welcome to Maranatha everyone. The real land of the free and home of the brave. Now before I let you go on inside there are two basic rules that everyone, and I mean everyone, follows in this camp. The first rule is that you do not steal. If you didn't bring it in or if someone didn't give it to you then leave it alone. We've kicked people out of our midst for stealing and as far as I am concerned none of you are any better than any of them. So, I warn you now. You get caught stealing, I don't care if it's a tick off a deer's ass, I'll kick you and your entire family out of here faster than you can say, 'So help me God.' Does everyone agree with and understand rule number one?" Kai waited for the answer which he received emphatically from the Hansens all at once as if they'd rehearsed it. "Well, alright. That goes for guests, too, gentlemen." Kai added looking into the truck's cab. "Rule number two, there has never, nor will there be any physical, sexual, verbal, or spiritual violence of any kind permitted within these gates. If you feel so inclined to commit such acts of idolatry you will do so outside of these hallowed walls. And if we uncover evidence that you have partaken in the perpetration of such acts upon the unwilling anywhere even close to these hallowed walls you and your kin will be kicked out faster than I can say..." Kai waited for the Hansen clan to respond.

"So help me God." The Hansens yelled in unison. Nick and Tommy both rolled their eyes. These people thought they were at a summer camp. The two men knew better. There were real monsters out there. Who knew how long the campers would have before they had their own close encounters?

"That's right. So does everyone agree with and understand rule number two?" Everyone answered affirmatively and Kai finished. "Once again, my name's Kai. Drive on in. Once you get inside if you have any more questions just ask for Melissa. You can't miss her. She's got a mop of fire hanging from the top of her head."

Kai waved the truck through. As Nick drove past the gates, the Hansen family waved and shouted at

Kai whom they obviously had gotten a real kick out of.

The distance between the front gate and the camp was much longer than Nick had anticipated. From a security standpoint, it was a smart thing to have such a wide gap between the two. Tommy mentioned something about them having to use expensive radios to cover such a distance. They must have driven a mile before the unpaved road opened up onto a wide dirt parking lot. There were at least a couple of hundred cars of all different makes and models parked in an organized manner in between the road and the camp. Nick, again, thought the placement of the parking lot was not only practical but could act as an incendiary buffer zone in case a violent provocation with outsiders were to ensue. Before Nick could park, a beautiful young woman with incredibly untidy red hair, which she slovenly tried putting into a bun, came out to greet them. She signaled for them to continue further into the camp. Much to Tommy's delight, Melissa jumped up onto the running board at the bottom of the passenger side door.

"Well, hello darling. Now you must be Melissa?" Tommy flirted.

"Yeah, Mr. Hansen, right?" before Amanda could correct her Melissa directed them to pull into a roundabout shaded by tall, low-hanging pepper trees.

"Wow, this place just keeps getting prettier and prettier by the minute," Tommy said trying for Melissa's attention again. The young woman just laughed it off and pet Arnold on the head. The bulldog looked back at Tommy smiling. Melissa then hopped down from the truck as Nick slowed down and parked.

"Okay, before you guys get settled in we have to get you all signed in," Melissa shouted so everyone could hear her. The Hansens lined up in front of the boat with their bags including Amanda who happily rejoined their ranks. Melissa checked them all in and then walked over to Nick, still in the truck. "Okay, guys. Our visitor policy is pretty strict. All visitors can spend one night without any conditions apart from the two rules Kai already told you about. But if you want to stay you will have to give us the keys to your vehicle. We know you're hunters and are armed but we also know that you helped our members tremendously. So, we won't go through and confiscate your weapons, but you can't return to your car until you're ready to leave in the morning. You've got to be out by midday tomorrow just like a hotel. Does that sound like something you guys can handle?"

Nick was about to speak when Tommy broke in lured by the woman's soft pale skin and the slight twang in her voice, "Absolutely, Melissa." Tommy confirmed. She smiled knowingly then continued.

"Okay, great, now if you'll just step on out we will set you up in a tent for two, excuse me, three and get you boys fed." Melissa finished.

"Sounds outright divine," Tommy added wasting no opportunity. Nick could only lower his head slightly embarrassed by his friend's shameless advances.

"My friend, here, has been hurt pretty bad. You guys have any wheelchairs lying around?" Nick whispered even though he knew Tommy could hear him.

"Absolutely. Hold on. I'll be right back."

Nick turned to Tommy who was sporting his trademark Cheshire cat grin.

"Well, if that ain't the brightest pearl in the sea?" Tommy said unabashedly.

"You might as well paint a big sign on your head that says 'I'm yours.'" Nick teased. "And why do you sound like you're from the south all of a sudden?"

"I do declare, Nick, I think I might have just found Jesus."

Nick punched Tommy in the arm. But Tommy didn't laugh. It was something in the way he spoke that almost made him sound serious. Nick shrugged it off knowing that it would take much more than a beautiful redhead to turn Tommy's recalcitrant heart into a contrite one.

Melissa came back with a folding wheelchair and set it up for Tommy just outside the passenger side door. She helped him out of the truck and into the chair. He looked over at Nick secretly sporting a sly grin.

"Why thank you, darlin'. I am truly grateful for such fine hospitality. My name's Thomas Riggle." Tommy extended his hand in friendship.

"Melissa O'Connell." She replied but when she grabbed Tommy's hand he kissed it. Melissa blushed not knowing what to make of the man who so confidently sought her affections. "It's Nick, right?" she asked looking through the cab at Nick who had already gotten out and was dusting himself off.

"Yeah," Nick answered feeling like a third wheel. Arnold had already run off to play with a Great Dane who had come out to see what all the commotion was about. The two dogs became fast friends as they frolicked among the wild grasses that grew about the camp's entrance.

"Alright, you guys take what you need and then hand me the keys," Melissa ordered.

Nick threw Tommy's backpack onto his lap trying to snap him out of his love-obsessed stupor. Nick grabbed his own bag before tossing Melissa the keys over the hood of his truck. She caught them expertly in one hand with a snap of her wrist.

"Wait here. Somebody will show you where you'll stay the night. I'll see you guys later at dinner." Melissa said as she slid her athletic body into the driver's seat of the truck and slammed the driver's side door shut. Without needing Nick to show her where the emergency brake was she released it, started the engine, and drove off.

Tommy was doing doughnuts in his wheelchair. Nick couldn't believe how quickly his friend's mood had changed. It had been a long, long time since Nick had felt anything close to what Tommy was feeling right now. He dared not rain too much on the guy's parade. After all, he had just lost Jasper, his cabin, and his legs in one night. So, Nick rolled with it and tried his best not to make a big deal out of Tommy's behavior.

A big chubby kid wearing a black heavy metal t-shirt, torn denim vest, and jean shorts walked up to the guys and, with about as much excitement as a child going to the dentist. He introduced himself as Francis. Francis was pudge all over. His legs alone could've fed a cannibal tribe for a week. He led the two men and their dog to a large yurt fully furnished with two cots, a small wooden coffee table, and a large wicker lounge chair. As soon as Francis had fulfilled his function he left mumbling something about dinner in an hour. Arnold wasted no time and jumped onto one of the cots claiming it as his own.

"Would you look at this place?" Tommy was astounded. He had never been in a yurt before. Its tall canvas walls and round shape gave the spacious interior a classy, Sultan of Brunei vibe. "I could seriously get used to this."

"Tommy, you just got here." Nick declared not ready to fall in line just yet. He wanted to know who was running the show and felt that trying to ask around during dinner would be inappropriate. He wanted to know more about the doctor Amanda had mentioned or at the very least find someone who could help Arnold with his stitches. "I'll be back. Keep an eye on Arnold for me." Nick stood at the entrance of the tent for a moment and looked back at Tommy and Arnold sitting together on their cot. He suddenly felt out of place. "I'll probably just meet you at dinner."

"No prob. I'll keep two eyes on him. They'll be closed but I'll be looking straight at him. Haha." Tommy laughed.

Nick left the tent and went looking for a woman named Clarissa. During their drive Amanda kept rattling on about how great a leader Clarissa was. She was the 'go to' person in the camp and it would be her generosity that Nick would have to kindle to help his friends get medical attention. He asked a couple of people who pointed him in the direction of a small house built from freshly cut timbers. The house was clad with a solar panel roof and was complete with a water purifier and an electric water heater. Nick was impressed. The door to the small house was open. A soft lantern hung from its jam. The light meandered outward into the warm evening air that grew darker by the minute. He walked in and saw that the interior of the house was an office. There was an older woman sitting at a desk who immediately looked up at Nick surprised to see a stranger this close to the heart of the camp without her knowing about it.

"Hi, there. I'm sorry I don't know you. How may I help you?" she asked politely putting down her paperwork to address the situation at hand.

"Hey, I'm Nick Camby. My friend and I gave the Hansens a ride down here from Julian. I was told that I could find Clarissa here."

"Oh. Well, sure. How nice of you." The older woman said with a smile. She got up from her desk and walked to the only other room in the office. She knocked on the door that was slightly ajar. "Clarissa! You've got a guest. He's an outsider."

'An outsider', Nick thought. He waited in the tiny reception room looking around at all the books and decorations. The place looked like it had been put together by a bunch of amateur designers who were part of a speed challenge, the kind that used to air on TV. Everything was in the right spot but nothing about the place seemed original, kind of how offices always looked and felt. A smooth and confident voice called him into the office. He went inside and sitting behind a desk was a woman who was both striking and formidable in appearance. The woman's beauty seemed bound up inside her like a tiger in a cage too small. Her hair was pulled back into a tightly woven braid and even though she wore a Maranatha t-shirt and jeans she might as well have been wearing a pants suit. Nick hid his attraction behind an awkward yet charming smile. His grin, coupled with the scars on his face, created somewhat of an alarming impression on Clarissa who couldn't quite place the moral fibers of his being.

"Hello, Nick. I'm Clarissa Walcott. Welcome to Maranatha." She introduced herself looking through him as much as at him.

"Hi, there. Well…this is quite the setup."

"Yes, a lot of planning went into this community. We take our member's trust and their values very seriously. Now, what can I do for you? The chow bell is about to ring and I have to inspect the arrangements. So, let's make this quick, shall we?"

"I understand. The Hansen's told me that there was a doctor in the camp. Me, my friend, and my dog all got attacked by a bear during a recent hunting trip." Nick said pointing to his face as proof of his lie. "We could really use a little looking after."

"Well, Robert Hansen is an extremely valuable member of our camp. He is our head of agricultural production and a brewmaster as well. Maranatha is extremely grateful that you brought him and his family safely to us. The least we could do is offer immediate care for your group. Now, normally, our doctors do not work after hours unless it's an emergency but I will make an exception in your case. Stay behind after dinner and I will coordinate a check-up with someone. Okay?"

"Sounds good. I appreciate it." Nick thanked Clarissa reaching out for her hand, more to touch her than to be cordial. She grabbed it forcefully.

Her hand was cold but soft. Nick noticed that she wasn't wearing a wedding ring and there was no tan line on her ring finger either. Even though he wanted to Nick didn't dare flirt with her as she seemed committed to Maranatha and little else.

"Don't mention it." Clarissa didn't have to excuse Nick. Her body language did the job for her. Nick sheepishly left the office. He hadn't expected to meet such a pretty woman without cleaning, shaving, or wearing the proper attire.

Nick wandered through the camp thinking of everything that had happened to him in the last two days. He took stock of the complex implications of the creature's existence. Dale's words kept playing over and over in his mind. Nick was desperately trying to weave a narrative that could explain the few pieces of information he had. Having come up short as to an explanation for the monster, Nick's mind began observing the camp which was now swallowed by a purple taffy-colored sky. He admired the simple beauty of the cows and goats grazing lazily in the nearby fields. Thunderheads could be seen far to the east. Their pillowy contours were lit by the occasional lightning bolt. A tepid breeze flew through Maranatha easing the anxiousness Nick was feeling.

Maranatha was shaped like a giant key. One long road stretched from the wooden cattle gate at the entrance to the camp to the dirt parking lot but from there it flared out and toured around the perimeter of a large campsite. Beyond the road, on the other side of the living quarters, a large-scale agricultural project was underway. The living areas and structures that had been built out encompassed an area of about fifteen acres, but the whole site, including the farming operations, must have been more than a dozen acres. Nick saw plenty of people rolling around on ATVs and electric golf carts keeping busy doing Lord knows what. He leaned over a wooden fence along the road to inspect the camp's septic system when the dinner bell began to ring. The tone of the bell brought back childhood memories of sixth-grade camp. Nick hadn't enjoyed his sixth-grade camp experience. He had been sick the whole time and the girl he liked dumped him for a tryst with a boy from another school. The emotions he felt then overlapped with his current situation bridging his past and his present in an unwelcome manner.

Nick followed a stream of hungry people instead of asking for directions to the canteen. Seeing everyone in the camp together in one place gave Maranatha an identity, a proportion. The canteen was timber and corrugated metal construction much larger than Clarissa's office. It was a row house with a giant veranda that paralleled its roofline on one side. Groups of generic manila and orange picnic tables took up a great deal of space in front of the canteen. On the other side of the tables, a giant fire pit made of faux lava rock rose several feet from the ground. Behind it, a matching stone wall had been constructed adorned with tropical plants and palm trees. The words 'Camp

Maranatha', cut from stainless steel sheeting and polished to a shine, had been affixed to the wall and backlit with LEDs. Nick thought the whole thing looked like something from a cheesy Hawaiian tourist brochure. Nevertheless, he respected the obvious effort that went into the camp's overall design.

Underneath the canteen's roofline, kerosene tray heaters warmed a long row of freshly prepared dishes. Nick grabbed a vacuum-formed metal tray and queued up like everyone else. He was pleased with the food being served. There were two different meat options and three different sides. Nick scooped a healthy spoonful of ground turkey lasagna and topped it off with a salad and two pieces of buttered garlic bread. He poured a powdered-based juice drink into his glass and went to find Tommy and Arnold but didn't see them anywhere.

Nick went off by himself and sat down at an empty picnic table which didn't stay empty for long.

He was soon joined by a bunch of eager teenagers who thought Nick was cool. Word had already traveled around the camp about two hunters, one with a giant scar. The young campers wanted to hear about Nick's fight with the bear. Nick fed their minds with a tale much more plausible than what had truly happened in the mountains. After he was finished, the teens introduced themselves and they all shared a few good laughs. Nick kept looking around for Tommy and finally caught a glimpse of his wheelchair bound friend sitting with a group of strangers. Tommy's hands were underneath the table feeding his dinner to Arnold who sat at his feet licking the dinner plate clean.

"Great," Nick thought. Arnold would be passing gas all night long. But something was off. Tommy never shared his food. The guy routinely ate enough for three people. He was about to walk over to his friend to jokingly question him about his appetite when he saw that Tommy was busy chatting up Melissa with marvelous effect. No wonder, he thought. Tommy was smitten. Nick wanted to be happy for his best friend. But the camp, the whole thing in Nick's eyes, was a lie, a pleasant illusion of safety. Looking out onto the campers of Maranatha, after having killed an alien being, was like looking into a fishbowl; but, instead of watching goldfish swimming around aimlessly, there were people eating lasagna and laughing it up. He wondered if any of them wanted to know the real truth, that dangerous lizard people were hiding in caves all around them. Nick looked up toward Signal Hill which overlooked the surrounding mesa. He wondered if it too harbored reptilian beings. He turned back around to the company at his table and made the best of things by asking as many questions of others as were asked of him. But not since his encounter with the huge portal had it once left his mind.

The dinner bell rang again and like good little sheeple, everyone gathered their trays and returned them to an array of large plastic bins underneath the veranda. As the herd filed out, Nick saw that one table of people remained. Tommy, Clarissa, Kai, Robert Hansen, and a few others beckoned him over. Arnold came running over to Nick with his tongue hanging out of his gaping mouth as if to say, 'come join the party'. He strolled over to the table squeezing in on the edge of one of the benches and smiled a smile that bordered on the uneasy side.

There was a little silence as the heads of the community shared glances before speaking. Everyone at the table then bowed their heads in prayer. Nick took the opportunity to exchange glances with Tommy but got irritated when he found that he, too, had bowed his head. Nick looked around in amazement. He felt as though something was happening right in front of him, but he was too blind to see it. The small group prayed to God specifically thanking Him for bringing Nick and Tommy into their camp; which didn't sound right to Nick. When Kai, who had led the prayer, ended it by saying "Amen" Tommy raised his head to see his friend staring at him in bewilderment.

"Well, Nick, I have asked the leaders of our humble community here to talk about your situation." Clarissa started.

'My situation?' Nick thought to himself.

"But, before we get started let me introduce everyone to you. You have met Kai Wagner. He is our director of operations and second in command. To his left is Birdie Johnson. She oversees facilities, mainly the canteen, but also many other things. God bless her. Next to her is Robert Hansen, our chief agricultural technician, whom you've met. I am the camp's director. I am also the lead veterinarian. I will be the one who stitches up Arnold later tonight. Next to me is Dennis Mulhaney. Dennis is a retired police lieutenant. He's in charge of all security measures here at Maranatha. And to Dennis' left is Pravit Ramjahd. Pravit is our horribly overworked technical advisor whom we simply could not do without. Together, our mission here at Maranatha is simple but requires our continual efforts. I am very proud of the team we've assembled here. And as you can see, a lot of planning has gone into making Maranatha a real home to our members, many of whom have not yet made it here."

Nick waved 'hello'. He was about to ask about the doctor when Clarissa, reading his mind, broke his chain of thought.

"I know you must be wondering where the physicians are. Well, it seems as though we won't be needing them tonight. So, I told them to get some rest."

"I am sorry. I just thought that you wanted us to leave by midday tomorrow. That doesn't leave much time for Tom..."

"Yes, about that, Nick. Tommy has expressed a desire to join Maranatha." Clarissa added leaving space at the end of her proclamation for Nick to fill in with his unsaid response. He gave it. There was no hiding his aggravation with Tommy. The news dropped on his ears harder than Dale's ramblings from the mine. He just sat there utterly perplexed. He looked at his friend whom he felt had just sold him out somehow. Nick understood it was selfish of him to be upset but he had really wished Tommy had discussed the matter with him first.

"Tommy is this really what you want?" Nick asked beseeching his friend who seemed to be growing more and more distant with him by the second.

"I love this place. I didn't talk about it with you before because I knew you would be angry with me." Tommy confessed placing Nick in an even more awkward position, the odd man out.

"Well, I think that's great. I, mean, this place is pretty awesome. But doesn't membership here require faith?" Nick mentioned hoping to put a kibosh on the whole situation.

"Tommy has asked to be baptized," Robert said smiling at Tommy who bowed his head in agreement. Nick was pissed now. He thought he could see through Tommy's cheesy ambitions. But now wasn't the time or the place to make a fuss about things. They were here to determine Nick's fate, a position of vulnerability that he hadn't asked for.

"Wow, that's incredible. Yeah, that's great." Nick responded not telling the truth. He was sitting atop his real feelings like they were a live grenade. "Tommy would make a great addition to your camp. He is, by far, the best engineer I have ever met. He is combat tested and can think outside the box while under pressure. He has my total support."

The entire group looked around the table pleased with Nick's acceptance of his best friend's newfound faith. Nick didn't know if it was fueled by the needs of Tommy's groin or if he was sincere. It may have been that Nick never realized just who

Tommy was. Either way, he wasn't sure what to do. He didn't want to go off on his own to fish Imperial Beach by himself. At the same time, he wasn't ready to have the God conversation.

"The truth is Pravit could use some help around here. By the sound of things Tommy could probably help Robert out a great deal as well." Clarissa said. "Which brings us to you, Nicholas. Tommy tells us that you are the best soldier he's ever met. He says that you can perform any security protocol necessary if called upon. And that you specialize in something called 'asset recovery', a term we have just become aware of. Is that true?"

"I am a well-trained combat operator but," Nick looked over to Dennis, "Dennis has made some pretty intelligent choices with the arrangement of this community. The parking lot situated in between the camp and the road is both functional and tactical. He's doing a great job. I don't know how I could add to his expertise. Besides, to be honest with all of you, I am not sure I am ready to join the faith as much as I admire it."

"We thought you might say something like that, Nick. But you're a good guy." Kai spoke up, "That's why we want to offer you a very special job. Dennis, would you do the honors? This is your neck of the woods."

"Surely," Dennis said repositioning himself on the bench. "First of all, Nick, I want to thank you for taking the time to notice the little details around the camp. I have already discussed this with Clarissa. Basically, we need more protection than we have. You see, underneath me, I've got about fifty guys out of this whole bunch that I know are willing to risk their lives in defense of this camp. But I need you to help train them and get them to be combat and patrol ready. Most importantly, I need eyes and ears outside of the camp. We'd give you a car, an ATV, and your own tent wherever you'd want on the premises. And you'd be the only other person, besides me, allowed to keep a firearm on their hip while inside the camp. Now how does that sound to ya?"

"It sounds like an offer I can't refuse. I mean, I, we never thought that we'd come across such a fine group of people out here." Nick professed. The generous offer settled into Nick's mind shrouding it with a silver lining. Yet, still, his heart was heavy. The desire to understand the truth about the creature wasn't going to go away. He knew deep inside his curiosity would eventually get the better of him. And just as the scar remained with him so did the memory of the lizardman's existence. As sweet as Dennis' deal was, he could sense that something vital to the conversation was being left out or danced around. Nick knew there must've been some other reason the Maranathans were extending such an invitation without needing to be converted. The ex-soldier didn't waste time putting his would-be betters on the spot. "So, what is it you're not telling me? There must be another reason you'd want me here without requiring me to join the church. What is it that you really want?"

The group all sat back and took notice of Nick's intelligence. They hadn't realized, until now, that he was able to perceive matters at such a level. Tommy just smiled knowing Nick wasn't the kind of mule who would move just because you dangled a carrot in front of him. Clarissa held up her hand to the others wanting to take the responsibility for whatever was said next.

"Every week we send a handful of volunteers out in a van to go on supply runs. We don't want to risk anyone from our security force because they are also our laborers. We target different areas every time that we deem to be safe. Two days ago, we sent a van out to Santee for a supply run and it never came back. We were lucky in the sense that the couple who volunteered to go had no other ties to the camp, no children, but we fear the worst for them."

"Surely, you were in radio contact with them? What happened?" Nick asked.

"They call themselves the Berserkergang." Dennis provided. "They are a motorcycle gang that has sent the Hell's Angels running for the hills. We believe their main area of operations is in Escondido. But when the government opened the prisons their ranks swelled and they have since spread further and further south."

"You want me alone to go out into the middle of a motorcycle gang to retrieve two people?" Nick questioned the group's logic, their sanity, "You are aware that people will have to die, right?"

"Now, now, just hold on there a minute, Nick. We have been in communication with someone at the gang's Santee hideout. They have made a list of demands that we are more than prepared to meet. What we need is someone to go out there and make the transaction, our people for a van full of medical supplies and dried food." Dennis said with a straight face.

"And there's the rub. You guys just wanna send me out there to die for you just like you sent that couple out there. Wow, how quickly society reorganizes itself. You're like the new capitol hill folk." Out of nowhere, a well of anger shot upward out of Nick. "Look, you all are nice people. I get that, but guess what? There is a world out there full of pissed off sons of bitches who now assume the government lied to them about the storms. And when they find you guys out here living like civilized good little sheep they are going to devour this place. You do realize that, don't you? This place isn't safe from what's coming. You can't protect people from the world they now live in. It's anarchy. There are no rules anymore."

The whole group absorbed the truth Nick spoke. No one could say anything to him. Nick stood up rippling with conviction. He looked dead at Clarissa, "I will do this for you willingly because I care about people and I want Tommy to be happy here, Lord knows he deserves a little happiness. But

Q. J. Zephyr

I served my country so that you and everyone at this table could have the luxury of imagining a place like this. Now, I'm not going mope around here holding my service record over everybody's head like some asshole. But don't you dare try to pull me around on a leash. If I ask for something I don't want any pushback. And, please, save me the pitch next time and get to the matter at hand. I'm no child. Now do you we have an understanding?"

"Yes, I believe we do. Thank you so much, Nicholas. I'm sorry if we didn't get to the truth sooner but we really do want to get Mark and Sarah back. I take full responsibility for what has happened. I'm sorry." Clarissa came in and gave him a hug, her eyes welling up. And when she let go she looked at him for the first time seeing the man Nick really was. She then bent down to put Arnold on a leash and walked him away. Kai came up to Nick next.

"I'd go out there with you, amigo, but I'm afraid I'd just be slowing ya down," Kai said patting Nick on the back. He thanked Nick and then sauntered off into the night. Everyone did the same. Dennis was the last to approach.

"What are you gonna need from me, Nick. Just tell me and it's yours?" Dennis asked having no other choice but to look up to Nick who stood tall at six feet two inches.

"The keys to my damn truck," Nick replied staring at Tommy who just sat there amused by the entire conversation.

Chapter 7: Trouble

Leila stared at her bare toes. They were filthy. Reddish mud had taken residence in her nail beds. She used her fingernails, which had grown quite long, to clean them out. Leila had enjoyed a very temporary popularity. Her newfound friends now only reluctantly acknowledged her presence. To make matters worse, Leila noticed that Marsala had stopped coming around to say hello. This worried the little girl who saw the woman as her adoptive mother of sorts. Leila put it in her mind to find out why and raised her tiny legs from her usual spot in the corner to seek her out.

Leila's act of bravery and defiance had sent waves of different emotions throughout the shelter. Most of the adults regarded her very coldly. Lots of people had been indirectly forced into skipping an important meal due to her little stunt with the reptilian guards. And so when she asked around for

Marsala she was unable to uncover any information regarding the matter. But Leila was determined and went off to find the one person who could find out for her, Jacob.

It wasn't hard to find him in the multitude of sorrowful people. He was in the middle of a crowd of dirty-faced teens who were making a big fuss about something. When Leila went to investigate she saw that Jacob was in the middle of a pushup contest with a much older boy and winning. Those who had gathered around were counting aloud. They'd all reached forty-two by the time Leila arrived. Jacob was strong for a twelve year-old and Leila tried to imagine what he would look like by the time he became her dad's age. The contest continued until the count reached sixty-five. Both the boys began to struggle greatly as their thin, toned arms strained to lift their torsos off the filthy floor. Neither boy was willing to concede. They just kept on. It was hard for Leila to watch. In the end, Jacob was able to manage two more pushups than his competitor who collapsed onto the ground in defeat. The small crowd began to chant, "Eat it! Eat it! Eat it!"

Leila looked around for a silver food packet but didn't see any. She was curious as to what the older boy was supposed to eat. Suddenly, another boy emerged from the crowd cupping something in his hand. He walked over to the loser and ordered him to stand up and open his mouth. The teenagers kept up the chant and then started screaming when a large cockroach was dropped into the loser's mouth. Leila could only look on in disgust. The older boy grimaced as he chewed and swallowed the insect down. Strangely, he was commended by everyone around him even more than Jacob had been for winning.

Jacob's chest was still heaving when he came over after seeing Leila. "Pretty gross, right? That's how I won. I just keep thinking about how nasty that thing was gonna taste. Haha!"

"I can't believe he did that. Boys are so weird. I don't get it." Leila said contorting her face. She kept thinking about the moment the roach's thin flailing legs touched the boy's outstretched tongue.

"A contest isn't worth winning unless there's a reward. And when there's no reward to be had, you just replace it with risk."

"Why didn't you just compete over food?" She wanted to know.

"Are you kidding me? That's even more of a risk than eating a bug." Jacob laughed. "Pretty cool though, right? I mean, beating an older kid like that. He's sixteen!"

Leila smiled and laughed shaking her head. She gave Jacob a high five. And the two of them walked back together toward Leila's favorite part of the shelter. "Jacob, where is Marsala? Why doesn't she come to say hello to me anymore?"

"She hasn't? I could've sworn I saw her go over to you a little while ago. But my memory is jacked up. I can't seem to remember things right. Time is blending everything together down here. When there's no yesterday or tomorrow how do you tell when anything happens at all? After it happens, I mean?"

Leila knew exactly what Jacob meant. "No, I haven't seen her since a little while after the last food drop. No one will talk to me."

"Yeah, well that's understandable. I think you may have actually killed somebody. Haha. So cool." Jacob smirked making light of the situation at Leila's expense.

"C'mon, Jacob. I'm serious. I'm really worried about her. Can you please find out for me what is going on?" Leila asked looking up to him as though he were her elder brother.

"Yeah, I got you. Just give me some time, okay." Jacob promised. "I'll be back."

"Okay." Leila agreed. She liked Jacob and thought he was handsome, too. She decided right

then and there that her first boyfriend would have
to be a leader like Jacob.

Leila remained in her dark little corner watching
for the tunnel to open to see if anyone new would
come tumbling through it. She had already
witnessed five people come out of the opening
since her arrival that she had been aware of. She
kept watch as best she could hoping her mother
and father would soon roll out of it. She waited in
vain.

When Leila was younger her father would take
her to Port Elizabeth to collect seashells that had
washed up on the warm yellow sands. Leila was
always amazed at the brilliant colors they
possessed. Her father told her that the creatures'
diets who inhabited the shells determined the
shell's colors scheme. He also told her that each
shell was often used by more than one creature and
that they would swap them out for better ones just
like people did with their cars and houses. Her
father loved the sea. Leila could tell by the way he

looked out onto the Atlantic. She used to imagine her father as a prince of an underwater kingdom who had emerged from the waves to find and marry her mother.

Coffee didn't like sand and so didn't travel to the beach very often. Instead, she would shop the many outlets that lined the Eastern Cape's boardwalk. She would often wave to her mother who would be eating shave ice underneath an umbrella while Leila and her father were drying off in the sun. Leila's mother was very beautiful. Coffee had come from a wealthy family and had the tastes and habits to go along with it. She used to say to her daughter that she had married out of money instead of into it. She advised Leila not to do the same because times were getting more and more difficult. Her mother wanted Leila to become a doctor like many other parents Leila knew. But Leila's mother, more than anything, didn't want her daughter to rely on anyone else for money or happiness. For this reason, Coffee taught Leila many things ahead of her time, like how to balance a checkbook. Whenever Coffee made deposits in the bank she would have Leila hand the money to the clerk who would kindly hand the little girl the receipt of deposit. Leila would have to verify the amounts and so the young girl developed a wide range of skills that made her ever the more unique.

The fond memories of her family lulled Leila to sleep. Thankfully, she didn't dream and caught up on some much needed rest. The rumbling in the walls woke her soon after. Through bleary eyes, Leila reflexively sought out the nearest waterspout. There were more people than ever before ready to drink. Leila knew she could only blame herself. She had mistakenly told Jacob the secret of the rumble who, in turn, told all the other children. She managed only one mouthful of water before being pushed to the floor by a grown man who sneered at her in disgust. After the man had satisfied himself he turned back toward Leila and began yelling obscenities at her. She could only back away from him on her hands and feet. He kicked Leila down to the ground, hard. Her head hit the floor with an audible thud pushing tears out of her tear ducts. Leila screamed for someone to help. She feared the man would kill her, or even worse, throw her into the hole which was now only a couple of meters away. The man grabbed Leila's gown by the sleeve and began to drag her toward the hole when a large, muscled arm stopped him. She couldn't believe it. It was the biggest man from the darkest corner of the shelter.

"No!" the large man commanded. But the smaller man, driven by rage and hunger, didn't let go of Leila and scoffed at him. It was a bad idea. The large man proceeded to head-butt Leila's aggressor repeatedly until his limp body fell onto the wet floor of the cell. The brute then lifted the man over his head and deposited him into the hole without the slightest bit of remorse. Everyone else inside the shelter had seen Leila getting attacked and had chosen to do nothing about it. Their eyes absorbed the consequences of messing with the large man whose intentions in protecting Leila were not clear to her at all.

"Thank you," Leila said through tears and a ringing skull but the large man didn't even look in her direction. He just returned to the corner where his brutish friends lingered. Leila ran back to her corner crying. She didn't understand anything or anyone. Nothing made sense to her and to make matters worse Jacob was waiting for her when she got back. He stood against the wall with his head down. Leila couldn't understand why Jacob hadn't come to help. Why hadn't any of the children come to her aid? She was furious.

She hit Jacob several times asking him why he had not tried to save her. She truly thought they had become friends. Jacob took the punches and continued to look down at the floor.

"Everyone wants you dead, Leila. Nobody wants you here any longer." He muttered. His words struck her like a wet blade.

"What are you talking about?" Leila cried. "I thought we were friends."

"We are, Leila, but it's more complicated now."

"I don't understand. What is going on? Why did that man protect me? I thought he was the bad guy in here?"

"Oh, he is. That's why I came over here. I need to tell you something. It's about Marsala. It's also about the food." Jacob finally lifted his head.

"Well, what is it?" Leila asked only interested in the topic of Marsala's sudden disinterest in her.

"She won't ever talk to you again."

"Why? It's because of what happened with the food? But why does that make her hate me?"

"She doesn't hate you. She loves you, Leila. The men in the corner own her now."

"What do you mean they own her? How can someone own another person? That doesn't make any sense." Leila crossed her arms. Her head was still throbbing from being slammed against the ground.

"There's no easy way to say this, Leila. Marsala has sacrificed herself to those men in the corner for the sake of all the children in here, specifically you. Those men have sex with Marsala any time they want in exchange for making sure that you and I have a chance at surviving. And it's not just Marsala. Three other girls are now sex slaves over in that corner. They're not allowed to leave for any reason. There's a water hole by them and that's the only time they can even get up to walk around.

"No!" Leila cried. She knew about rape from watching detective shows on television. She didn't know what it looked like or felt like, only that it was when a man forced himself on a woman.

"Yes." Jacob lowered his head. He didn't want to stay friends with Leila anymore. She had only brought more pain into the shelter. He walked away knowing that his withdrawal would completely isolate her. He no longer cared. Jacob had formed a crush on one of the older teenage girls the men were now abusing. He was frustrated in that, short of dying himself, there was nothing he could do to save her.

Leila slid down into a deep depression. She curled in the fetal position, tears spent. She could only see the filth of the shelter's floor and the dirty feet that trod upon it. Her heart was emptied, crushed, and it was all her fault. The thought of Marsala sacrificing her body for her sake was so far beyond Leila's scope of life experience that it brought new understanding to the young girl. Everything had a price, she thought, a risk, a reward, and a repercussion. She lay on the floor for a long time. The next food delivery came yet Leila still did not move. A pair of large feet approached her and dropped a single shiny food packet in front of the girl's motionless eyes. Leila didn't take it. For her, the food packet was but a symbol that stood for her complicity with the injustice of Marsala's treatment. Leila felt that her life wasn't any more important than Marsala's. Everyone deserves to live. Everyone. Her conviction began to build inside her. She sat up and threw the unopened food packet near the hole in the middle of the floor. Noticing her abandon the meal, an elderly woman crept up to it like a spider and took ate it ravenously in front of everyone, unashamed.

Leila racked her brain. How could she get rid of the big man in the corner? Leila knew that if he was gone things would get better, especially for Marsala. She began to plot and scheme for a way to free Marsala. For Leila, nothing was off-limits to her imagination, the ways justified the means so long as her friend was freed. The young girl refused to live in a world where abuse, perversion, and avarice ruled. She decided that she didn't care if she died in the process of delivering Marsala from enslavement. She was going to do something about it. That's when the idea came to her. And it was just crazy enough to work. She would eventually need

Jacob's help. The first thing she needed to do, however, was practice jumping.

The other people in the shelter considered a child doing calisthenics to be both odd and stupid, a waste of calories. But Leila was focused. She ran the little distance she could before leaping as far she could. She trained continuously only stopping to sleep. Soon, the young girl could cover two meters easily and that was all she needed. The diameter of the hole in the middle of the room was only a little longer than she was tall. Once she was confident she could cover the distance of the hole in one leap she looked for Jacob who was more curious than anyone else as to what she was up to. She found him arguing with a girl about something trivial when she asked him to have a word. Jacob agreed. She pulled him away to one of the places inside the shelter where no one could hear them.

"You love Megan don't you, Jacob? I, mean, you would do anything to help get her out of that corner, right?" Leila asked him about one of the girls who had volunteered themselves to the brutes. She had found out her name by promising one of her meals to an older lady who used to sit by the girl in the shelter.

Jacob instantly blushed and answered angrily, "What do you want Leila?"

"I know of a way, but I need your help. Yours and all the other children you can get together."

"Oh, yeah? Why should I help you? You're just a pain in everybody's ass."

"Because if you help get rid of the big guy guess who'll think you're a hero?"

"And what exactly do you suppose we do, huh?"

"Well, I'll tell you but first you have to promise that you'll help. If you do, I'll promise no one else but the big guy gets hurt. Deal?" Leila asked reaching out her hand. Jacob shook it. She whispered her secret plan to him and he nodded in approval. Jacob then walked off collecting a couple of empty food packets from the floor on his way to barter for loyalty.

Leila spent the next couple of weeks trying her hand at a crude form of chemistry. Her plan called for creating a super slippery substance with whatever she could find. She tried many different combinations but found marginal success. On the floor in her little corner, Leila practiced making a concoction that first required dried urine. Then she put a mixture of spat mucus on top which made the substance pretty slippery. But the viscosity still wasn't right. The mucus couldn't be spread out as much as she needed and was too thin. She decided to wait until the next food drop to try adding oily food to the mix. She was sure that it would work. When the next food drop came Leila grabbed three packets off the ground. She ended up having to snatch one from the hands of another girl who cried and walked off not wanting to fight her over it. Leila kept her promise and gave one of the packets to the old woman who had provided her with Megan's name. The other two she needed for her experiment.

Leila went back over to her corner and poured one of the packet's contents over the dried urine on the floor. It was much more slippery but still, Leila thought, it could be better. She didn't want to take any chances. She struggled with what else to add. As she sat and contemplated an idea struck her like a bolt of lightning. Leila remembered a time when she was eight years-old and sick as a dog. She had thrown up on the tiled bathroom floor in her home and then slipped on it hitting her head against the rim of the toilet bowl. Feeling inspired, Leila downed the remaining contents of the opened food packet and waited patiently for a while. When she was sure what she had eaten had been partially digested she threw it back up and into the empty food pouch. She then poured its contents over the dried urine and achieved the desired slipperiness she was sure was necessary to pull off her plan. She had almost slipped herself which was a great sign.

Q. J. Zephyr

It was time to go to the bathroom. Leila knelt just in front of the hole holding the extra food pouch in her hand and began to urinate. She had chosen the exact spot wisely as it faced the direction of the brute's corner. Her stream laced the floor around the hole forming a thin puddle. She walked back to her corner nonchalantly disregarding the remarks others had made when she purposefully missed the mark. She sat down and watched the urine dry. It took a while. When it did she was ready. She went to Jacob to let him know that it was time.

The big man in the corner, whose name was Byron, slept like a male lion, all the time. Since there was no night or day, people fell asleep when their bodies told them to. Leila waited for the man to stir from one of his naps. One of the older girls, whom Jacob had enlisted to help, signaled to her that Byron was getting up. Leila quickly scrambled to the patch of dried urine and spread her slippery concoction on top of it with her hands. She signaled back to the girl who attempted to seduce the large man by hiking her gown up and calling out his name. Groans of lust flowed from the group of men like apes during mating season. Byron heard the commotion and upon seeing the voluptuous curves of the girl brought him out of his corner. He invited her into his protective circle but she gestured that she wanted him to have her right there in front of everyone. He obliged but as he hiked up his gown to reveal himself Leila, and a handful of other children, flagged his entire body with a combination of the most repugnant bodily effluences imaginable. The young temptress scurried off revealing Leila's lone, frail person standing in front of him. Leila screamed obscenities at him and called him out for being a monger in front of everyone. She called him every foul name she could think of to bait him, and it worked. Covered in gunk, Byron thought nothing of the deal he had struck with Marsala and raged after the little girl who bee-lined it straight to the hole in the middle of the room. Like a gazelle, she jumped just before the slippery part on the floor in front of the hole making it to the other side easily and safely. The brute, filled with the hubris of his own physicality, ran straight into Leila's trap and slipped knocking blood out of his brow as he hit the floor. Byron slid into the hole headfirst, but to Leila's amazement, he managed to clamp his hands down like two vices onto the edge of the hole, his muscular body dangling. He yelled for his comrades to help, but much to everyone's surprise they held back and did nothing. Leila ran back around to where Byron's hands had grabbed hold and was just about to pry them open when Jacob, like a white knight, stormed in out of nowhere. With the dexterity of a professional footballer, the boy slide-tackled Byron with enough force to knock his powerful grip loose. But Jacob had overcompensated and his slide carried him to the point where the full length of his legs dangled over the edge of the opening. Byron grabbed onto Jacob's legs in sheer desperation. The brute started

The 9 Orders: The Collection

to climb up Jacob's body like a rope ladder. Jacob couldn't support the man's weight and began to slide down into the hole. Leila grabbed one of Jacob's arms from just beside the slippery spot and used all her strength to pull him free. She screamed for help, but no one came.

"Please! Help us! Somebody grab a hold of me! Please." Leila continued to scream. No one did anything. They just watched Jacob increasingly lose his grip. Their mouths hung open and their eyes wide, the people in the shelter were completely taken in by the spectacle. It was as though the entire thing was taking place on a movie screen.

"Leila." Jacob looked up at the little girl. His eyes were filled with sadness but not fear. And as Byron's arm encircled Jacob's neck the young boy spoke, "Kiss her for me." Jacob let go of Leila's arms not wanting to drag the little girl down with her. The two bodies plummeted down to certain death. There was only silence. The entire shelter was rocked to the core. A wave of indescribable wrath, born from the roiling madness of the shelter, filled Leila with a hate so strong that she stood up and cursed everyone in the room.

"Cowards! Idiots! Vermin!" Leila shrieked at the top of her lungs like a witch casting a binding spell. Her words clung to the guilty like stink to a sewer. "All of you deserve to die! All of you will die! Every last one of you will die in here. None of you will ever see the light of day. How could you?"

Leila yelled until her throat gave out. She then ran over to the corner where the other 'tough men' stood. Without their alpha male, they were no stronger than any of the other cowardly men in the shelter. Leila ran past them without a glance and into the arms of Marsala. The men did nothing. Leila and Marsala cried together walking away from the corner and its horrible memories. Leila could say only that she was sorry. She promised Marsala that she would be safe. The other two women left the corner as well. And Megan, now free, was the only person to walk over to the hole and cry for Jacob. She wasn't a fool. She knew the young boy had a thing for her. She caught him stealing glances at her almost every five minutes. She wept in honor of his sacrifice.

Jacob, Megan, Marsala, Leila, and the two other women had all sacrificed themselves and as a result, changed the very spirit of the shelter. It went from being a hell on earth to a manageable diminishment of freedom. For every reward a risk, for every risk, a repercussion became Leila's newfound philosophy. It would be forever etched into her heart by the death, sacrifice, and the love of a boy named Jacob.

Chapter 8: The Drop Off

"I cannot believe you did that, man," Nick complained while in the privacy of the visitor's tent. "You made me look like a total fool, like the Grinch or something."

"I don't think so at all. You saw the way Clarissa looked at you. I can tell you have the hots for her by the way."

"This whole thing is funny to you, isn't it?"

"A little. But, look, Nick, nobody is twisting your arm here." Tommy declared. "You can go fish the dirty waters of imperial Beach if you want to, but I'm staying put."

"I don't see how you can be so calm about joining this camp after what we've experienced."

"There is nothing we can do about what happened. I mean, what are you gonna do? Go back into that mine with a winch?"

"You know, now that you mention it, that's exactly what the hell I'm gonna do. I can't just sit on my ass like the last two days didn't happen." Nick paced back and forth thinking of what he would have to take with him to return to the door, open it, and be brave enough to enter into it by himself.

"You're crazy, Nick, and you're acting like a friggin' child," Tommy said switching gears, moods. "The fact of the matter is everyone is screwed. We're all screwed. Those who registered and those who didn't and that's without the knowledge that reptilian predators are living in the mountains of America! Your best bet for survival is to surround yourself with people you can trust. I've met a lot of assholes, Nick, and these aren't them. This place is as safe as anywhere, which I know don't mean nothin' to you, but when was the last time you ever tried gettin' around without using your legs, huh? So, corncob me up the wazoo if I see fit to want to be somewhere safe while I try to regain my damn manhood!"

"No, that's not what this is about!" Nick flared. "I want you to get better more than anyone. Why didn't you talk to me? Why didn't you come to me first? That's what this is about."

"What's done is done, my friend. Get over it. I played a card and it sunk the jackpot. And just so you know, they didn't say anything to me about going after a vanful of dumbasses when I asked them if I could join Maranatha. Let's be clear on that. And don't think that your going after 'em has anything to do with making me happy because that's a decision that you're making on your own. But you and I both know that that is the price of admission when you don't wanna play by their rules, now don't you? So, go fish the damn ocean. Take my boat. I don't give a rat's ass but don't drag me along in your glum like some limp dick superhero sidekick."

"How can you say that, man? You're unbelievable. This is all about you. This whole thing is all about you, Tommy. Truth is, you didn't care about what I would do or what would happen to me when you made your decision. That's why you made it without me." Nick was hurt but washed it down with a canteen full of water. "Look, I don't want to talk like this with you anymore. It's pointless. I don't want to go to IB alone. But I don't want to be here either. After I return from this 'op', which I'm gonna need your help with, by the way, I'm going back up to those mountains to open that friggin' door if it's the last thing I do on this earth."

"Which it may very well be..." Tommy interrupted.

Nick continued without breaking for Tommy's remark, "And after I open it, I'm going to get answers. I don't care if I have to go it alone. At this point, I don't even care about coming back at all. I want the truth. I can't live in this, this…fish bowl knowing what I know now."

"Fine by me. Where would you like me to sign on your death certificate?" Tommy asked showing the whites of his teeth without smiling. Nick's desire to return made Tommy feel sick to his stomach. In the end, he would blame himself if anything ever happened to Nick. In Tommy's mind, his intentions had been pure. He wanted Nick to have a life and to feel as though he was needed, useful. He thought that forcing Nick into joining Maranatha would be good for him. He was wrong.

"Very funny." Nick grinned on his way back to being his normal self, but he made a last-minute detour that led to the mindset he would have to cultivate for his mission in recovering the camp's kidnapped members. "I'm gonna need you to make three grasshoppers for me. I need to tie them underneath the van they give me."

"If you set three of them off in one place it'll blow a crater the size of a Volkswagen underneath whatever that van is parked over." Tommy pointed out. His signature explosive had been nicknamed the 'grasshopper' because, if triggered, it sent people's bodies flying tens of meters in the air in the direction of the blast. And as the dead carcasses flew through the air they looked like grasshoppers hopping about.

"I'm counting on it. I'll go pull the truck up so we can get to work. I'll be right back."

"Okay. I'm not going anywhere." Tommy said laying back on his cot. He looked around for Arnold but forgot that he was still getting stitched up by Clarissa.

Nick returned with his truck and parked it next to the entrance of the visitor's tent. He went to the back of his Ford and started hauling out all kinds of stuff Tommy could use for making his explosives. He also set his gear up for the mission laying out everything he would need on the carpeted floor of the yurt. It took Tommy until morning to finish making the grasshoppers. He then went straight to bed. As if in shifts, Nick woke from a short nap. He had tried to stay up thinking that he was finally going to memorize the steps it took to create Tommy's mayhem masterpiece. But after the engineer had soldered his twelfth circuit, and they still were only on the second explosive, Nick fell asleep. It was time to get a move on. Nick pushed aside the flap of the yurt and went looking for Dennis who was most likely performing an early morning patrol around the camp. The rising sun spilled over the eastern hills and the calming sounds of the people stirring from sleep sang through the cold morning air. Nick eventually found the retired policeman gassing up an ATV behind the canteen.

"Good morning." Nick offered his salutations lifting his trigger finger to the invisible brim of a nonexistent cowboy hat.

"Morning, Nick. I take it you're ready."

"As I'll ever be. Let's get the finer points ironed out. I'm gonna need to retrofit the van a little too before I leave."

"Sounds good. The van's stocked and ready to go. I'll have somebody pull it around for you." Dennis radioed one of his many subordinates to retrieve the vehicle. "I don't know how this whole thing is gonna turn out. I've never been in this kind of situation before. I really don't know how much help I can be to ya."

"Look, Dennis. Let me spell it out for you. This operation will go one of two ways. Either everyone dies, including your members, or I return with them unharmed. I know that isn't saying much. But I can guarantee you that is how it will play out. If they harm them or try to renegotiate the terms of the deal, they're dead. Pure and simple. That's how we do things in the desert. The only difference is we don't have drones or air support."

"Oh, I've got a few drones. I didn't even think of using them. There's no video obviously 'cuz we don't have internet, but the range for their remotes is about a half-mile with a vertical climb that can reach just over two hundred feet. Do ya want one?"

"Hell, yes!" Nick started thinking through all of the drone's possible applications. He wouldn't be able to use it for reconnaissance unless he strapped a camera onto it and that just sounded like a pain in the ass to him. But he could use the remote flyer to blow stuff up. "I'm gonna need a whole lotta string. As much as you can give me in one spool. Oh, and gimme some extra batteries for it, too, just in case."

"I know you probably like traveling light but several of our guys, upon hearing of your involvement, have volunteered their services. Is that something you might be interested in?" Dennis offered, "I tried to tell 'em that they'd probably just get in your way, but they want to help. In the event you do succeed I don't think they want you hoggin' all the glory around camp. The hearts of men, huh."

"Can they shoot?" was all Nick wanted to know. He could use sharpshooters. What mission couldn't benefit from having them?

"Well, I got one guy that I'm pretty sure can hit a tin can from a hundred yards but he's definitely not up to SWAT standards. Two other guys I don't know, but they seem pretty scrappy to me." Dennis stated trying to remain truthful.

"I'll take 'em. Put 'em in the ugliest most inconspicuous car you've got. Tell them to be ready in an hour."

"Roger, that. I'll be in my tent with the CB when you're ready. We'll contact the biker gang together and then you guys can get going. But first, you need to eat breakfast."

"No. No food for anyone that comes with me. Operations are conducted on empty stomachs. You don't have time to take dumps. Are we clear? No one is to eat anything. Just make sure they're hydrated."

"Gotcha. I'll tell the men. Their names are Roger, Frank, and Lindo. They'll be with me in my tent whenever you're ready."

"Good. Let's get this ball rolling." The van pulled up and Francis got out. He slovenly walked up to Dennis handing him the keys to the van. Dennis observed the kid with a minor degree of disdain and gestured for him to hand the keys to Nick instead. Nick took them and drove the van back over to the visitor's tent.

After Nick finished zip tying the grasshoppers onto the van's undercarriage he became curious about its cargo. He pulled himself out from underneath the vehicle and went around to its back doors. He opened them he couldn't believe what he saw. Jugs containing the essential properties needed to cook and cut up meth were stockpiled inside. Nick was beyond livid. How arrogant of the leadership of the camp, he thought. Did they think he was so naïve as to not know what he was looking at? Was the camp's leadership so unaware that they blindly fulfilled the biker gang's demand without even knowing what the chemicals could be used for? Either way, it sealed the deal in terms of Nick leaving after the mission was over. He slammed the van doors shut and went back inside to get geared up and say goodbye to Tommy, who was still fast asleep.

Nick marched over to Dennis' tent in a huff. On his way in he saw a bronze-colored Chevy Nova parked outside. It was a perfect ringer. Nick decided he wasn't going to say anything about the van's cargo. If anything, he could use the volatile chemicals to his tactical advantage. The Ford Sprinter was now literally nothing more than a massive bomb on wheels. Nick barged into Dennis' tent ready for action. The three men that were going to accompany him on the mission were standing off to the side waiting. Nick acknowledged them and then turned his attention to Dennis.

"Call 'em up," Nick ordered. Dennis set everything up and looked at Nick before speaking. Nick signaled for him to go ahead.

"Breaker, Breaker, 214. Breaker, Breaker 214. Looking for Nimrod. Looking for Nimrod. Are you out there, Nimrod?" Dennis coded waiting patiently for a response. He got it within seconds.

"Go for Nimrod." A thin, devious voice sounded on the other side.

"This is Archangel. I repeat this is Archangel requesting the location of the drop, over."

"Santee Municipal Airport 1300 hours. Repeat, Santee Municipal Airport at 1300. Copy that?" The voice responded.

"10-4. The drop is at Santee Municipal Airport at 1300. We have the supplies you requested. We will be there. What condition are our members in?"

"They're alive. Over and out." With that, the communication ended. Dennis put down the mic and picked up a bunch of walkie-talkies. He handed them out to Nick and the others. Frank, who Dennis pointed out as the best shooter in the camp, requested an earpiece instead. As Frank fitted the device onto his person Nick gave Roger and Lindo a once over.

"You two think you're brave enough to handle driving the van onto the tarmac and making the swap without screwing up?" Nick asked.

"What? You want us to..." Lindo responded.

"Absolutely." Roger, an obvious hothead, broke in.

Nick closed in on Roger and Lindo. "There is no Maranatha. You're a community located in National City, nothing more than a few neighbors who've banded together. Everything that you have, you have to search for. You're a bunch of weak-willed scavenger types. You got that?" Nick questioned them. "You and Lindo can't be armed. It won't matter if you are because they will pat you down at the beginning of the transaction. Make sure you don't say anything other than what I have just told you. Don't even move unless it's to pick the assets off the ground and put them in that ugly ass car outside. Are we clear?"

The two men both agreed hesitantly. "Frank," Nick continued, "I don't know the layout of the airport. We're gonna have to go in early and find a good place for you to nest."

"Sorry to interrupt you, Nick, but I'm pretty sure I've got the plans for the airport in those flat files over there."

"What? You gotta be kidding me? You're just full of surprises, Dennis. Bring 'em over here."

"After the government shutdown, I broke into my old office and took the plans for every major civic structure in the county in case the weather got bad. Thank God we haven't had to use 'em at all. I figured they weren't going to be needing them anymore."

The 9 Orders: The Collection

Dennis fingered through several stacks of plans in the flat files until he pulled out a tall roll held together by a single purple rubber band. "Here it is. Santee Municipal Airport stamped 2021. Now, that's the last time they built onto that site. I remember because I have a friend who stores a plane out there and he was really happy that they added two extra hangars on the south end of the airstrip."

"I like you, Dennis. I like the way you think. Strong work." Nick gave the older man his props as he unrolled the plans onto a worktable in the middle of the tent. He poured over the blueprints pointing out key features to the four men at his side. He was able to visualize where he wanted to position Frank whose accuracy and range defined his proximity to where Roger and Lindo would park the van during the drop-off. Nick would conceal himself behind a set of cooling vents on the top of the now-abandoned control tower. He had no idea how he was going to get up there, but he would find a way. The key to a successful mission was to recover the assets and exit the tarmac as quickly as possible. Nick explained to Roger and Lindo how they were to handle themselves when they came face to face with the bikers. He instructed the men to stand outside of the vehicle with both arms raised keys in hand. All the doors of the van should be opened for easy inspection. He assured the men that if they played their roles right the bikers would leave well enough alone and ride off with their haul. But, if things went south, Nick told them to recover the assets at all costs and to then put as much distance between themselves and the van as possible. He stressed the point again without further explanation. Everyone seemed to understand. Nick didn't want to let on that he intended to blow the van filled with chemicals sky high. After he was finished going over the rough details of the game plan with everyone, Nick took Frank aside walking him out of the tent for a private chat. Nick wanted to get a feel for the men that could make or break the operation.

"Frank, how well do you know the other men?" Nick asked openly.

"Not, well, sir."

"Sir? Are you a veteran?" Nick asked stepping backward.

"Yessir, I was a Lance Corporal in the Marines. Did two tours in Syria before I got medically discharged for PTSD1."

"Hallelujah! Man, am I glad to have you." Nick took a slightly different stance when he processed the man's admission to being diagnosed with the most aggressive form of combat fatigue. He put his hand on Frank's shoulder. "How are you holding up considering all of this?" Nick asked shaking the man's hand. Frank was average-sized, balding, and built the same way someone would build a robot, maximum efficiency with minimum weight.

"Thanks to the Lord Jesus Christ I am past the worst of it, sir. But I can't seem to outrun the nightmares or the electric skin."

"Hmm. I see." Nick replied knowing all too well about the condition caused by being exposed to too many bomb blasts and nerve agents. He had been diagnosed with the same disorder, but instead of meeting it head-on, as it appeared Frank was doing, Nick drank himself to a point so close to death that he and the grim reaper had become drinking buddies.

"Look, Frank...let me be honest with you. Those guys in the tent, not Dennis, but the other two are most likely going to screw this thing up. It's almost guaranteed they will. So, when things go south and the bikers scatter or try to harm the principals, I want you to start taking out those closest to your people. Don't worry about anything else because I'll be with you downrange. Okay?"

"Yessir. I'd like to thank you for letting me participate in recovering our members. But I have to ask you for a favor, sir" Frank said.

"I may be Army, but my father and my grandfather were both leathernecks. You name it and it's done, brother."

"Thank you, sir. I would ask that we pray before we leave." Frank requested following Nick back inside the tent.

"No problem, Lance Corporal. But you should be the one who does the talking." Nick suggested impressed by the man's demeanor, stoic but genuine. It was refreshing to be around

The five men prayed together in the solace of Dennis' tent. When they were done Dennis hugged every man, showing them a great deal of affection. Nick asked for one more car just in case. Roger and Lindo would drive the van, Frank would take the beat-up Nova, and Nick led the way in an older blue Dodge Neon. The caravan drove out to the airport taking their time along the way. Nick was confident the bikers wouldn't be setting up a perimeter this early in the day. They were probably too busy sleeping off the drugs and stupor from the night before.

Nick had the guys park a quarter of a mile away from the airport. They scoped the site using binoculars making sure they were the first ones there. They were to search for anything or anyone out of the ordinary. The airport, like most of the city, was barren. Nick gave everyone a few last-minute instructions before sending them to their positions. He remained behind to view the van's entry onto the tarmac. Its arrival might provoke the movement of a lookout in hiding. He also wanted to make sure Frank couldn't be seen from the freeway.

After successfully parking the van in the middle of the airfield, Roger and Lindo radioed that they were good to go. Nick instructed them to ditch their walkie talkies in a nearby trashcan but to leave the mics on standby by using duct tape to the squawker depressed. Nick was hoping the open channel might distract any eavesdroppers away from the closed channel he intended to use with Frank. He then told the two men to just sit there and wait with the doors and windows of the van open. Nick turned his attention to Frank's position. The marine was well hidden. Nick switched his vantage points several times and couldn't make out Frank or his rifle. Satisfied with the placement of the others it was time for Nick to get to the top of the five-story control tower.

Nick drove behind a large warehouse adjacent to the airport and parked the Neon up against the nine-foot chain link fence that surrounded the airfield. Nick got out and jumped onto the roof of the vehicle using it to aid his ascent. He lowered his pack, filled with the gear he would need for the day, gently onto the ground on the opposite side of the fence. He nimbly jumped over and crept toward the tower where he spied a locked maintenance door containing a small rectangular window. Nick broke open the pane of glass in the door before reaching inside the opening and unlocking the door from the inside. He entered locking the door behind him before climbing the staircase leading to the roof.

When he made it to the top Nick looked around. He took in all he could see from his perch. The airport was a poor place for the gang to have chosen for the dropoff. The control tower was the tallest structure for miles around and the land that surrounded the airport was flatter than a pancake. Nick started to set up shop. He removed the drone from his pack and rigged two grenades to it using the string Dennis had given him. He tested the drone and was thrilled to see how well it handled the added weight of the grenades. Nick attached a string to each pin then connected them both to the spool. He envisioned flying the device high over the heads of the bikers once the deal went off the rails. True to his word, Nick was prepared to kill everyone last one of the bikers if anything happened to Mark and Sarah.

Dennis had given Nick one of the couple's cellphones so Nick would be able to identify them. He scrolled through the phone's photos and determined that it belonged to Sarah. But as he scrolled through the image gallery he noticed less and less of Mark and more and more of Roger. Nick surmised that Roger and Sarah were having an affair unbeknownst to poor Mark. It was most likely the reason Roger had volunteered for the mission and why Nick had pegged him for a hothead. Roger was an emotional powder keg. Nick's intuition told him things could only go one way, bad.

The brilliant midday sun baked the roof of the control tower like a heat lamp. Nick had to retreat into the shade of the ventilation stacks several times to escape the rising humidity. Waiting amid such high temperatures proved to be much more of a challenge than Nick had bargained for. He desperately wanted to hydrate but had only brought enough water for the kidnappees. He radioed Frank who confirmed that he was fine. Roger and Lindo were making the most of their wait. They had fallen asleep in the van, engine running, blasting the AC. Suddenly, Nick heard the distant growls of motorcycle engines coming from the east. He put the binoculars up to his eyes and beheld a long chain of bikers descending upon the frontage road that led to the airport.

"Look, alive Frank. Here they come. Get ready." Nick radioed.

"Copy that," Frank replied. "I see them."

Nick could only look on and hope that everything went well. He wanted to return Mark and Sarah to the camp unharmed. He wondered if circumstances would conspire on their behalf. Nick was curious to see if Frank's prayer would grant them any more luck than fate had already allotted them.

The 9 Orders: The Collection

Roger and Lindo sat up startled at the sound of the mighty trail of Harleys that began encircling the van like hungry vultures over rotting carrion. They both got out of the van like Nick had instructed, arms raised, and keys in hand. At least forty bikers whirled around the two men in an over-the-top display of intimidation. The bikers eventually parked their hogs enclosing the van in a circle with a thirty-foot perimeter, nice and tight. Their leader, still donning his ecru prison jumpsuit, had a scar around his neck from an obvious attempt on his life. He was as scruffy as they came and stood tall at 6'6". The ex-con was tatted all over the place, except on his face. He didn't say a word and just ogled the heck out of Roger and Lindo, sizing them up. The two Maranathans were dressed very ordinarily giving the leader of the Berserkergang the impression that maybe they weren't taking anarchy and those who served under its flag seriously enough. The large man slowly walked over to inspect the van's cargo nodding his head in approval. He then walked over to Roger, who held the keys in his left hand and began breathing down the young man's neck. He licked Roger from his clavicle up to his forehead leaving a slimy trail of tobacco-scented saliva all over Roger's face, yet the young man did not move. Nick, observing the showdown through the scope of his rifle, was amazed. He had misjudged Roger by making him out to be a loose cannon. But Roger's calm reaction to the biker did everything to strengthen his suspicion that he had been sleeping with Sarah.

The large man grabbed Roger by the hair and yanked him backward making him face the blazing sun. But the man only grabbed the keys before walking back to his beast of a machine. Mark and Sarah were sitting side-saddle on the back of two of the gang's choppers. Their mouths, arms, and legs had been duct taped. The big man gestured for his soldiers to make the exchange. But as Roger and Lindo began removing the tape from Mark and Sarah's legs the leader held up his forefinger, covered in Celtic tribal symbols, and spoke in a voice that sounded like someone trying to start a lawnmower, "Wait. I just have one question. Where'd you get the supplies?"

Roger, seeking any opportunity to prove himself, spoke up before Lindo could even think of something to say. "We salvaged what we could from the harbors. There's a naval base over by 32nd street. I don't know where there's more. It took us a few days just to find what you wanted. Now can we please go? You got what you came for." Roger asked in a surprisingly even tone for someone whose lover lay bound and bloodied before him.

The leader of the Beserkergang thought for a moment. Roger could tell the ex-con was deciding whether or not to kill him. There was no way for the felon to know that there were two sights aimed at his skull. All the bear of a man had to do was just let Roger and the rest of the Maranathans go and everything would be fine. But some men don't like to play by the rules even when they're the ones that make them. Some men were born to defy everything, even themselves. The leader of the gang was one of those men.

"Yeah, they can go. But not you. No, you're going straight to hell." The leader of the biker gang raised the muzzle of a shotgun that had been attached to the side of his rig and aimed it right at Roger with the full intention of blowing a hole the size of a grapefruit in his abdomen. But Frank was a vigilant man and from more than a hundred and fifty yards out pulled his rifle's trigger just seconds after the shotgun had been brandished. The leader's brains were blown clear out of the back of his skull splattering his grey matter all over those closest to him. The rest of the gang could only watch as the man's giant body fell backward against his bike, arms outstretched like he was being beamed up by a UFO. In a matter of seconds, the calm exchange turned into a chaotic scrum of gunfire and obscenities. Frank continued to snipe the men closest to Roger and Lindo who were now running as fast as they could from the van carrying Mark and Sarah in their arms. The four Maranatha members eventually made it safely behind one of the hangars on the south end of the tarmac. Nick, having witnessed the tension develop, had already flown the drone into the air above the heads of the bikers. They were so busy shooting off into Frank's direction they failed to see the tiny angel of death hovering above their heads. Nick positioned the drone over the van and tugged at the length of the string with the perfect amount of force needed to pull the pins from the grenades. He then cut the power to the drone and watched as it crashed onto the van's roof. A handful of the bikers turned around seeing their doom spelled out in front of their eyes. Without so much as a word to their comrades they tried in vain to speed off on their bikes, but it was too late. The explosion lifted the van twenty feet into the air and sent shards of red-hot axle rocketing outward in every direction. The radius of the blast was enormous and the bodies of dead and dying bikers were thrown into the air like rag dolls in the hands of an angry child. The control tower's windows warbled and shattered as a powerful shockwave passed through Nick and continued outward toward the frontage road shaking the fencing that guarded the airport's perimeter. A single biker managed to avoid being maimed after being thrown off his bike. He staggered up as quickly as he could lifting his dented and scraped chariot off the ground. He frantically straddled his bike and twisted the ignition key one too many times. He had flooded the engine. The irate biker threw the useless bike to the ground and made a break for it. Nick set the man's head in his sights and picked him off as cleanly as if he were a petal on a daisy.

Seeing that the Berserkergang had been neutralized Nick gathered his things and ran down onto the tarmac. There were survivors. Nick could see their mashed up limbs reaching out for help. Alive or not, Nick shot every one of those bikers in the head. After he was satisfied that the site was secure he radioed Frank to come out and drive the Nova over to where Roger and the others were waiting. Frank didn't answer. Nick radioed again but there was no response.

"Roger! Lindo!" Nick yelled. "Come out! Hurry up. It's over."

The two men came from around the side of the hangar with Mark and Sarah in tow. The woman had been violated. Rivulets of dried blood caked her inner thighs to her ankles. Her husband had been beaten to the edge of consciousness and could barely stand on his own two feet. They were in bad shape but would live. "Get them out of here now. Take the Neon. I parked it over there behind that yellow dumpster." Nick said pointing in the intended direction. "Drive as fast as you can and make sure there that nobody follows you. If anyone does drive toward the coast and then use this somehow."

Roger grabbed the 9mm Nick had picked up from one of the dead bikers then asked, "Where's Frank?"

"I'm gonna go check on him now." Nick was about to run off but stopped to shake Roger's hand, "You really played your role well today, Roger. I thought you were gonna lose it when that guy licked you, man, but it turns out you're cool as a cucumber under pressure. You too, Lindo. Now get your people out of here, fast. I'll ride back in the Nova with Frank."

"Alright. Thanks, Nick. You and Frank saved our lives today." Roger said. Lindo nodded his head and shook Nick's hand as well. Nick dipped his chin and took off for Frank's nest located on the opposite end of the airstrip.

When he got to the Lance Corporal's position the man was still lying among the brambles with his weapon aimed downrange. "Frank! Frank!" Nick went over to him and placed his hand on the marine's back. He knew instantly that Frank was dead. He rolled the man's body over to check for bullet wounds and strangely found nothing. He carefully searched Frank's person looking for any signs of trauma. Nick saw that Frank's collar had been saturated by something wet. Nick unzipped the collar only to find a pinkish wire mark dug into Frank's neck. Someone had strangled him using an incredible amount of pressure. That meant whoever it was had repositioned Frank's body to lure him. It had worked. Nick cursed himself for not sweeping the area first. Before he could even look around a man jumped down from a nearby pepper tree and slammed into Nick's back with the force of a falling anvil. Nick hit the ground bruising a couple of ribs in the process. The trained soldier recovered quickly but not before he found himself inside the most brutal stranglehold he'd ever been in. Thankfully, Nick had managed to slip his gloved hand in between the biker's garrote and his neck. Nick tried Judo flipping his assailant off his back, but his foe was stubborn and as strong as an ox.

The man backed himself up against the trunk of the pepper tree and dug his heels into the ground.

"You killed my brothers, my family. Now you're gonna die, you son of a bitch. Die!"

The biker must've been on PCP, Nick thought. His sustained endurance was off the charts. Like a constrictor, the pressure the man was applying to Nick's neck seemed to exponentially increase with every breath he took. Nick was losing consciousness and his vision began to blur. His military training kicked into high gear. There was an old trick a retired Green Beret had taught him. Nick inhaled deeply and held as much oxygen as he could within his diaphragm, not his throat. He tried his best to remain as calm as possible. A lesser man would've been dead already. Nick reached for his handgun, inverted his wrist, and shot behind him two times with no effect. He knew the bullets hit the man in his ribcage. He had felt their impact but still, the stranglehold tightened. In a last ditch effort to save his life, Nick placed the gun in between his legs and shot two more bullets up and backward. The man immediately let go and Nick head-butted him twice with the back of his pounding skull. Nick pushed his legs against the tree trunk and felt a flash of white-hot pain in his right thigh as he rolled away from his attacker. Nick had accidentally shot himself in the thigh. The bullet had done more than graze him. It had ripped a small chunk of his flesh off, a small price to pay for remaining alive.

The ex-soldier whipped around as fast he could hoping for a kill shot, but the toe-headed biker lunged at him expertly knocking Nick's gun out of his hand. The two of them tussled on the ground trying to gain dominance over each other. Nick simply could not get the guy off him. Nick threw a handful of loose sand and gravel into the man's eyes. Unphased, but without his sight, the biker rained down a series of chimpanzee-style hammer fists onto Nick's head and chest. The biker was giving Nick a serious run for his money. Nick knew he had to end the fight. He went for the knife in his boot, but the man tracked Nick's thoughts and pinned his arm down with one of his knees and one of his hands. Perfect, Nick thought, seeing a golden opportunity. He sat up to his left and snaked his body around the man's outstretched arm while at the same time rolling across the man's muscular back. The weight of Nick's body forced his adversary into the fetal position. Nick continued his grappling movement by winding his leg around the underside of the man's right arm. His enemy knew an armbar was coming but could do nothing to prevent it as Nick sunk his grip in by straightening his powerful legs. CRACK! The sounds of the man's arm shattering should have signaled the end of the fight, but it didn't. The gnarly biker freed himself by pulling his arm completely out of socket. Both men stood up. Nick was woozy and the biker took advantage by ramming his head into Nick's chest like a raging bull, pinning him up against the pepper tree. Arm dangling, the biker backed away from Nick and desperately searched for the gun he had whacked out of the soldier's hand. That was all the time Nick needed. Nick reached down again for the knife in his boot and flung the seven-inch folded steel blade into the man's forehead with devastating accuracy. The knife drove its way deep into the man's cranium, its hilt almost touching his tanned leathery skin. Pistol half raised, the biker fell to the ground in a bloody heap. Nick gasped and dropped to his knees. He had to catch his breath. The fight with the biker had nearly taken everything out of him, including his life. Nick never saw the guy coming, a mistake that Frank, too, had made. The man must've been a lookout because Nick didn't see anyone from the circle of bikers leave. The guy had somehow slipped into hiding when the bikers first arrived and traced the shots that had brought down his comrades back to Frank's position.

Nick took a moment to appreciate his enemy's dead body then spat on it in disgust. Even though the biker had ingeniously used Frank's body as a ploy, he was also a drugged out loser with no self-respect. Nick was extremely proud to have ridden the world of him. He knelt beside Frank and felt the need to commemorate the marine's sacrifice. Nick found himself saying a small prayer on his behalf. He then closed Frank's eyelids for the last time.

Nick struggled to carry Frank's lifeless body back to the Chevy Nova. The pain from his bullet wound hounded him to no end. He felt honored to be personally escorting the man who saved the mission back to Maranatha. It had been Frank's decisive shooting that allowed Nick the time he need to set up the drone for impact. In Nick's eyes, however, the operation even though outwardly a success, had been a failure. He would have preferred to have swapped Frank's death with Lindo's or Roger's. A good shot was worth a dozen willing men. But Nick was sure that Clarissa and Dennis would be more than happy with the outcome of the situation. Hopefully, Frank's death would teach Maranatha a lesson or two about whom they chose to send on supply runs in the future.

Chapter 9: No More

The shelter remained free of dispute and, thankfully, no new people had entered the chamber. Marsala and several other adults inside the cell had dictated its new terms loosely but with finite perimeters: no violence and the children and the elderly ate and drank first. That was it. They had kept it up and it wasn't long before the living standards greatly improved. People started doing humane things like disposing of empty food packets and the digested contents of their stomachs in the hole instead of wherever was convenient. The rank odor, still pervasive, had lessened considerably and smiles could often be seen here and there.

Leila was still regarded with a ten-foot pole. Seeing what the little girl was capable of, coupled with her damning words, words that she could not take back, created a wall between her and everyone else, except Marsala. Leila remained at Marsala's side at all times. The little girl refused to let any further injustice come against her. Leila spoke very little and smiled much more. She did, however, have many deep conversations with Marsala in the safety of each other's company. They shared stories about their families and got to know one another intimately.

Out of nowhere the hatch to the shelter began to squeal as it opened. Everyone turned around to view the entrance. It was much too soon for another food disbursement. They had just eaten two water cycles ago. Whatever the lizards were going to do once they entered would be a new experience for everyone.

Six reptilian guards, all magnificently colored, stomped into the cell holding long metal poles that emitted twittering blue lights at one end. The leader of the cadre held an electronic tablet in his clawed hands. It began to project images onto the highest part of one of the shelter's walls. Five faces were displayed in high definition. Leila was one of them along with Marsala, Megan, and the other two women who had volunteered themselves in the protection of the children.

"Come forward." The lead guard spoke in perfect English. He repeated the command in Afrikaans without skipping a beat. The people in the shelter's mouths dropped open in shock. It was the first time anyone had ever heard the lizards speak. Those whose faces had been projected on the wall came forward slowly, fearing the worst. The reptilian guards stepped closer to Leila's small group and with a twist of their poles lassoed them around the neck with some kind of electrified band.

Leila tried to speak to Marsala but when she did an excruciating electric charge screeched through her tiny body forcing her tongue to remain still. The lizards laughed at the young girl's reaction to their restraining device before escorting her out of the shelter first. The other guards and the rest of their captives passed through the open portal, one in front of the other. Once they had all passed through, the hatch was shut with a distinct tone of finality. Leila could barely make out the muffled cries for freedom coming from within the shelter's thick walls. She smiled. The cowards inside would no longer be afforded the luxury of having her or the three other women around. They would have to continue onward into the darkness and uncertainty to live, die, or become nothing more than the animals they truly were.

For the first time, Leila could see that the shelter she had been in was one of the thousands. The cavernous space that housed the formidable dungeons seemed to continue forever. Leila could not see their end. The sight was breathtaking. How could all of this have been built underground, she asked herself? The place wasn't a bunker, it was a city. Numerous lizards were walking about completing tasks everywhere the eye could see. Digitized mechanical sounds, steam venting out of thermal turbines, and the wrenching and slamming of hatch doors could be heard throughout the underground facility. The entire place was lit with deeply saturated red light. Even though Leila knew she was no longer in hell the red lights gave her every impression that she was. She knew her father and mother were alive inside one of the many shelters. She could feel their presence in her heart but calling out for them would have been useless. The small group was led down an extremely long gangway that forked up ahead. Much to Leila's dismay, the group split as well. Megan and Leila went to the right on an incline. Marsala and the other woman were taken off to the left, their path descending further into the belly of the underground city. They could only wave goodbye to each other and mouth the words 'I love you' and 'Goodbye'. Leila wanted to cry but held back her tears. She didn't want to attract any more attention to herself.

Leila and Megan were taken into a large holding pin filled with dozens of other children of all ages. They were let loose from their electrified bonds and locked inside without a word of explanation as to what was happening to them.

"What is this place?" Megan asked once the doors had shut. "Hey, how long has everyone been in here?"

"You should know better than to ask that?" An older boy's voice quickly answered. "A while but not too long. Since I arrived three groups were brought in before the both of you." The boy was Megan's age.

"Have you been given water since you've been here?" Megan asked grasping for some kind of a timeline.

"Yes. But you can't think that way in here." He replied pointing to a rectangular fountain in the corner of the room. Megan looked at it and was filled with both relief and frustration. She was happy that water was readily available but now had no frame of reference for how long they would stay in the holding area.

"How many times have you been fed?" Megan continued questioning the boy who didn't seem to mind at all.

"We haven't been fed."

"Where do you go to the bathroom?" Leila asked the boy who looked at her and smiled not realizing that the young girl would have such a commanding voice.

"There." The boy gestured to the corner of the room. "But you can only pee. There's nowhere to poop. And I haven't seen anyone do that in here, yet." The boy understood that Megan and Leila were trying to use the body's process of hydration and digestion to sketch out a rough sense of how long the boy had been inside the holding pen.

"That's good! If you haven't been fed and there's nowhere to poop...then that means we won't be in here that long. I hope." Megan figured. Leila nodded her head in agreement.

"Wow, you two are pretty sharp." The boy replied. He came closer to the two girls. He was of mixed nationality, possibly Spanish and Italian or something close. Leila thought he was handsome but not as handsome as Jacob had been.

"What do you know about what's going on?" Megan cut to the chase.

"Nothing. What do you know?" he asked in return holding out his hand to whoever would shake it first, "My name's Logan."

"I'm Megan and," She took his hand firmly and shook it once, "This is Leila."

"Hi, Leila." Logan waved. "What are you like, twelve, eleven?"

"Ten," Leila answered.

"Oh, you look older, but I guess the shelters will do that to you." Logan smiled. "I'm only seventeen but one of the kids in here thought I was a thirty year-old man. Haha."

"What do all of us have in common? Why have we all been put into a room together? Megan asked. "Tell me what happened to you?"

"Everyone, shut up and listen!" Leila barked much to the astonishment of the children. They slowly gathered around Logan who began to speak.

"Well, I don't know. Everybody rolled into the shelter through a tube, right?" Logan asked. Everyone nodded their heads. "There were about two hundred people in there when I first got there."

"They were only forty in mine." Another child spoke.

"What? There had to be a thousand people in mine." Added yet another voice.

"After being there a while," Logan continued "it became obvious that there was a hierarchy inside. You know, people you had to deal with if you wanted to eat, drink, or live. But in my shelter, there were these three guys that wouldn't even let people crap into the hole without their approval."

Everyone gasped at the thought. "They weren't big guys, either, but they were crazy as hell. They killed anyone who crossed them. At some point, I knew that I would be the next to die. I gathered all my allies together and waited for a chance to strike back. Finally, as two of the men slept, we saw our opportunity. I strangled the third guy who stood watch and we threw him into the hole. Then a handful of us knotted our gowns together before tying them around the ankles of the other two while they were still asleep. Then we dragged them screaming and cursing into the hole, one by one. It took six of us to do it. After we killed them, things got a lot better for us. We used the bathroom whenever we wanted and everyone seemed to get something to eat whenever the crocodiles delivered the food."

"Crocodiles?" a group of seven or eight children asked at once in astonishment, hands on their hips.

"They're not crocodiles, they're dinosaurs!" one of them spoke. Everyone laughed realizing that there were lots of different names people called the reptilian guards. A small argument ensued as to the nature of the lizardmen. After the short inconclusive debate quieted down, the matter was interrupted by a sharp-witted little boy.

"If all that's true then why aren't you naked?" he asked.

"Haha. In our shelter, we stripped the dead taking their gowns before throwing them down the hole. We washed the gowns in water as best we could so that we could change once in a while." Logan answered. Megan and Leila just looked at each other in amazement. Neither of them had ever thought of doing that.

"Did everyone in here improve their shelter somehow?" Megan asked the group. Every last youth in the holding pen nodded their head. So that was it. That was the common denominator. Leila understood what Megan was thinking and was pleased. It possibly meant that they would be allowed to live, but to what end.

Suddenly, part of a wall retracted into itself revealing a corridor large enough for the group to enter single file. Leila was happy to be moving on confident that she and the others would not have to return to the shelters. They filed into the tunnel without being prompted. Human will and the desire to be free drove them forward. Up ahead Leila could see the tunnel split. A lizard was standing at the foot of the fork directing each gender into the corresponding corridor. When it was Leila's turn to walk forward she did so with courage.

Leila stepped through a wide portal that had long thick strips of plastic hanging down from it and into a large shower facility lit like a fitness center. Many girls were waiting in lines to take showers. Leila queued up in the shortest line and watched the few girls in front of her get undressed, throw their mucky gowns inside a square metal framed hole in the wall, and shower. Tingling sensations danced all over Leila's body as the cleansing steam of the showers reminded her of home. She focused on the streams of reddish water draining from everyone's dirty bodies to keep from becoming homesick. Megan came up from behind Leila and tickled her back. Leila had never seen someone so excited to take a shower before. After Jacob's death, whenever Leila looked at Megan, and her long, beautiful twisting locks, she couldn't help but think of Jacob's bravery. She had never kissed Megan for him. She didn't think Megan deserved it. Had she ever even thought of him once since he died?

When it was time for Leila to shower, she let the hot water pour over her. Her muscles softened and her shoulders slouched. She let go of a bladder full of urine that she hadn't realized her body had been feverishly holding onto then washed her hair for the first time since arriving at the shelters. After she was done, Leila stepped out of the shower area and was blown dry along with a few other girls by giant blow dryers fit into the jambs of the showering room's exit. Arrows on the floor, lit with a pale green light, directed them into another smaller room. She did not wait for Megan. She could see the girls in front of her entering the room with hair and leaving with buzz cuts. Leila couldn't help but laugh as she regarded the weird head shapes of many of the girls. Everyone seemed pretty unhappy about having their haircut so short but Leila loved the idea.

She entered the room thinking a lizard barber would appear and was a little disappointed when no one came. Instead, she was prompted to sit and place her head against a padded headrest on a bizarre-looking chair. She obeyed. A mechanical arm with a vacuum attached to its end began sucking, cutting, and siphoning Leila's hair. When most of her mane was gone the vacuum arm disappeared and a bowl-shaped cap lowered onto her head. In a few seconds, the machine quickly gave her a buzz cut. The cap retracted upward and Leila's head and face were again blown by fans removing any excess hair. She was prompted to exit by another green arrow pointing in the direction of another room. Leila left the hair cutting booth feeling as light as a feather. She felt like dancing. She kept rubbing the top of her head in amusement. Her short hair felt smooth and baby soft. When she went into the next room there was another line of girls waiting for the next stage of whatever it was that was happening to them. They were all relieved to find out that everyone was simply being dusted with delousing powder. That's when Leila heard screams of joy coming from yet another larger chamber just ahead of her. All the girls already inside it were incredibly happy about something.

Finally, it was Leila's turn to go into the room with all the excited girls. She smiled as she saw what was driving them so crazy. Inside a warehouse-sized room were vats of clothes of all kinds. There was a bin for jeans, jackets, shoes, and underwear. For the girls, it was the closest thing to shopping they had experienced in a long time. She observed the others trying out various outfits before settling on one. Unlike the others, Leila chose clothes for practical reasons. Comfortable undies, a pair of blue jeans, a cool t-shirt with one of her favorite bands on it, and a cool jacket, the kind that only boys wore. The clothes had been washed but whoever did hadn't used fabric softener, which would have been nice, Leila thought. Some of the other girls agreed with her. The clothes, even though clean, felt rough and over-starched against their newly washed skin.

There was only one exit out of the room and just to the side of it, Leila saw something that surprised her. Standing well over six feet tall was a female lizard. Leila was inextricably filled with joy. Her unsaid theory about the reptilians secretly helping the children in the shelters seemed truer than ever. The female's coloration was drab compared to her male counterparts, but she looked every bit as fierce. Her face was smoother than the males of her species and so were her scales. Leila went straight up to her stopping several feet away and regarded her with amazement. Leila understood that if the lizards could both articulate themselves and treat their opposite sex equally then how bad could they be. The guard grinned at the little girl and then spoke in a voice that sounded much like a human man's but with softer, more rounded tones at the back end of her intonations.

"You must be her."

"Who?" Leila laughed. The reptilian guard called into the following room in what could only have been their native tongue. It sounded garish but surprisingly familiar. A few moments later a male guard with stooping broad shoulders answered her call. Upon seeing Leila, the male guard's eyes narrowed.

"Come with me." He ordered Leila in a very somber manner. For some reason, Leila pictured the guard as a mechanic. He looked like a creature who had spent his entire life bent over machines. He was not a grand physical specimen, compared to even the female guard she had just seen, but Leila knew he was still most likely capable of great acts of strength.

The other girls watched Leila disappear ahead of them. Leila followed the lumbering reptilian who dragged himself through a disorienting array of stairs and corridors before stopping in a room that looked like a control center in a spy movie. There were many smaller reptilians manning computer monitors. Leila thought it ridiculous. Aside from the eerie red lights, the smaller reptilians looked like they were in a galactic call center. They muttered into headsets and typed weird characters onto the screens in front of them. The smaller reptilians looked nothing like the guards. They did, however, share the same olive green complexion as the female guard and were also very smooth in appearance. Leila quietly chuckled because there was nothing aggressive looking at all about these smaller reptilians. The little girl didn't understand if they were just younger than the guards or a different breed of reptilian altogether. On the wall facing the smaller lizards was a vast array of monitors each filled with an odd range of moving colors.

"Wait." The beast uttered before marching off. Leila dared not defy the guard's words. She may not have been in the shelters any longer, but she was very much aware of how vulnerable she was.

After the guard left Leila eyed the array of monitors. As she observed the odd colors shift she began to recognize familiar movements. The screens were displaying human beings but in a visual spectrum that was decidedly inhuman. The people on the screens were inside the shelters. She went numb. She desperately tried to search for her parents but couldn't make out the identities of the moving color blobs. She was no closer to her parents than she had been while inside the prison. The feeling of being so close to something that you desired but so far away pierced her. The guard returned with a much taller creature. Leila instantly recognized him. He was the one with the hood from the surface with the scary yellow eyes. He was carrying a backpack stuffed to the brim. It looked like a small pouch in the creature's grasp. The two reptilians stood before Leila speaking to each other before the one with the hood spoke. Leila noticed the creature with the hood had a long, muscular tail, unlike the guards she had come in contact with.

"Do you remember me?" He asked. His voice was much like the guard's but more hollow, cavernous.

"Yes," Leila answered. Her fear of the reptilian resurfaced. There was something different about him. He wasn't like the others. He was infinitely more dangerous.

"The first time I saw you I knew you would be dead in two weeks." The hooded creature paused. "You were more than weak. You were everything that I hate about human beings. But then something in you changed. We all could see it. That is when I realized that I had been wrong about you, about all human beings. You are strong. You are like us. You have fear, but you know how to use it. I will give you a chance, little one. It is a gift that I will never again give to another human again, so be grateful. This bag contains everything you will need to live on your own for a single lunar cycle. Take it and leave. Never return."

"I don't understand. What are you saying?" Leila could barely speak. She was gripped by the dark aura of the hooded creature's physical dominance. "You are taking me out of the shelters just to throw me into the storms. I want my mom and dad. Where are they? Please let us all go."

The hooded reptilian said no more and gave the pack to his subordinate before turning around and walking away through a portal and into another part of the facility. Leila was happy he had gone. She hadn't realized just how scared she was until he had left.

"Follow me." The guard commanded. They walked away from the control room for what seemed like an eternity before the guard eventually stopped in front of an elevator. He pushed a code into a number pad on the wall beside it. When the elevator arrived the lizardman gestured for Leila to enter inside. She obliged and turned around not knowing what to expect. The guard threw the bag into Leila's arms, the force of his throw pushed the young girl against the back wall of the elevator. He did not enter.

"Why? "Why are you doing this? I'll die up there. What about the storms?" Leila asked looking the creature straight in his beer-colored eyes.

"Your own leaders have done this to you. Fear not. There are no storms. You have been freed. Follow the moon to the east. Do not venture north! Do as the captain says and never return." The guard spoke. Sensing that the elevator doors were about to close the lizardman turned and began walking away. Leila, sensing a small trust between them, lunged forward thrusting her arm in between the lift's doors.

"But what are you? I mean, are you aliens? And what about my parents?" Leila questioned the guard. After a brief pause, the guard turned and looked over his hunched shoulder.

"We are the true Terrans of this planet. We are Setians. Your mother, your father are no longer living. Now, go little one." the creature gestured for Leila to go back inside the elevator. She slowly walked to the back of the elevator, slid down its wall, and fell to the floor. The doors to the elevator closed severing Leila from the horrible reality of the shelters.

The lift rocketed upwards at an amazing speed. Leila could do nothing but stare at the elevator's polished aluminum veneers. Was it true? Were her parents really dead? The lizardman could have just been lying, she thought. Either way, the news capsized the joy freedom was supposed to bring. In its place emerged a numbness. Leila simply could not grasp her situation. Her poor little mind was being drawn and quartered by a world she had been thrown into against her will. Had her parents simply listened to her in the beginning none of this would have happened, she thought. But there was no anger only sadness and the gravity of the rising elevator.

The stooped guard said there were no storms. She would soon see if that, too, had been a lie. Leila's ears began to pop. There was no telling how far down she had been. When the elevator stopped and its doors finally parted again, they opened out onto a maintenance corridor of a building. Leila poked her head out of the elevator like a meerkat investigating its surroundings. The building was completely silent. Leila exited the elevator. Its doors quickly closed behind her. At the same time, a partition rose from the floor and concealed the presence of the elevator. She scrambled around the room tugging at the few doors that were there. Only one was unlocked. She burst through it and stumbled into an empty underground parking garage. Leila ran, an instinct, she had not been able to exercise while underground. She ran up and out of the complex. She came to a security gate that had been firebombed, a charred jagged hole had been left in the middle of it. It was large enough for a person to climb through and so she did. She walked the steep ramp that led to the street and breathed in fresh air for the first time in a long time. Her heart was resuscitated by it. She breathed in the clean oxygen as if she were an astronaut returning from space. Her nose was met by the scent of the many things she had missed: flowers, salt, grass, and soil.

There were no signs of life anywhere. She walked up a nearby hill to gain a better view of her location. When she got to the top her knees buckled. She had to sit down and held onto a street sign for support. Leila became overwhelmed by the sight of the setting tangerine sun to the west and a waxing quarter moon to the east. South Africa was a beautiful place to behold. There were no electromagnetic storms, but it was pretty hot. There was no ruin. The government had lied to everyone. Leila wasn't sure how long she had been underground, but it had been long enough for whatever was supposed to have happened to occur. Her parents, Jacob, and countless others had all died for nothing. Leila wanted to know who was responsible. The reptilian guard said something about human leaders being responsible but how could that be?

Leila saw the name of the building she had just emerged from. The words Bank of Pretoria crested the marble building's façade. The letters seemed dead without electricity to make them glow brightly against the evening sky. The unlit sign mirrored how Leila felt inside. It was as if she had just been spat out of a dragon's stomach. She realized that even though she was truly free of the shelters a part of her missed them. She understood that being surrounded by people, no matter the conditions, was its own kind of certainty. The comforting voice from her dream had made good on its promise to deliver her from imprisonment but the part of the dream where she freed her parents had been a lie, or maybe, a misinterpretation. Yet, Leila's heart remained tethered to the belief that her parents might still be alive somewhere below ground. Despite the guard's assertion of their passing, she could still feel their presence, their connection to her. Leila offered up a prayer for Coffee and Richard infusing it with as much spiritual power as she could summon. She then prayed for God to show her the truth so that she would not be taken in by the lies of others ever again. The young girl stood up, legs still slightly trembling, and raised her bright face to the heavens. She put her skinny arms through the straps on her backpack and started walking east toward the rising moon.

Chapter 10: Return

Nick took his time driving back to Spring Valley. He had put the dead marine in the front seat with him propping him up as though he were alive and well. Nick knew that when he returned to Maranatha he would be greeted by a welcome party. But when they saw the cost of their revelry the campers would all have to shut their mouths and lower their heads, an intended effect. Maybe he was being too hard on them, Nick thought to himself. But the campers needed to understand that their little fishbowl was nothing more than an illusion. As far as Nick was concerned until he had answers there would be no peace for anyone, anywhere. Why had the government lied about the solar flares? What exactly was the reptilian? And why did Dale say the things he had before being remotely killed by a strange device embedded in his hand? And, by God, what was on the other side of that door? These were the questions that ate away at Nick's mind. In a way, they were driving him mad. The worst part of it was, his best friend in the whole world, who had experienced the same things he had, seemed totally committed to living in a state of denial.

Nick felt betrayed by Tommy and insulted by the ignorance of the campers at Maranatha. They were children, he thought. Even though he liked Dennis, he now knew how ill-prepared the man was to safeguard the camp against its potential aggressors. Maybe Tommy would recover and help train the campers after Nick had gone. In any event, Arnold would have to stay with Tommy in Maranatha. There was no way he would sacrifice his bully especially after seeing how happy he was playing with all the other dogs around the camp.

When Nick pulled up to Maranatha's gate he wasn't surprised to see Kai waiting for him. The tall cowboy moseyed up to the driver's side with his usual swagger. But when he bent down to offer his appreciation he saw Frank's lifeless, pallid face. His mood immediately changed. He could do nothing but lift his cowboy hat off his head and stare into the ground.

"I was afraid something like this was gonna happen." Kai mumbled, "What kinda shape are you in?"

"I'm lucky to be alive right now, Kai." Nick admitted, "The guy that killed Frank came real close to putting two notches on his belt."

Nick lifted his neck so Kai could see the mark the biker's wire guillotine had left on his skin. He then showed that Frank had the same mark around his neck.

"The guy was on angel dust. I shot him four times and he still didn't stop trying to kill me."

"Well, they're all waiting for ya. I guess there's no sense in radioing this in. Wouldn't do much good anyhow. Alright, brother, head on in. We can't thank you enough for helping us out. I'm sure Mark and Sarah, once they're better, will have a lot to say to you along those same lines."

"Your camp won't have any more problems with those bikers. They're all dead, every last one of 'em. Thanks to Frank here. He's a real hero, Kai. Make sure everybody knows it and doesn't forget it."

"You got it. Thanks again, Nick, from the bottom of my tin can heart." Kai said tearing up.

Nick accelerated driving the long distance down the road that led to the camp. It was a peaceful afternoon. A warm breeze flowed through the open windows of the Nova. Nick looked at the tall grasses swaying to and fro. He smelled the cow dung as if for the last time before driving through the parking area. When Nick pulled into the roundabout the entire camp was out there with signs that read "Jesus Loves You", "Thanks Nick", "Praise God" and more. The cheers began as soon as they saw the grill of the old junker pull up. Nick had never been praised for killing anyone before. His father had served in Vietnam. He remembered him telling stories of people spitting on him as soon as he got out of the plane after doing three tours. Nick's dad would have been extremely proud of this moment, more for the people themselves than for Nick. But their cheers subsided as soon as they saw Frank's body jostling awkwardly in the front seat. Nick parked the car and got out. No one swarmed him. Instead, they just looked inside the car at Frank not understanding if he had been seriously wounded or was dead. Frank's wife, a woman named Beth, rushed out to the Nova screaming bloody murder. Nick tried to put his arms around her but the woman snubbed his condolences. She opened the door hastily and the weight of her dead husband's body fell through her arms and onto Maranathan soil. Several of Frank's closer associates quickly came over and collected the man off the ground and carried him away from the horrified stares, the signs, and the shameful fanfare. Beth followed never taking her hands off her husband. She made no condemnations but gave no praise either. In the end, she was the sole person that had to pay the price for the leadership's fallibility.

Nick left the keys to the Nova inside the car and started to walk off toward the visitor's tent when he was met by Arnold on the way. He was so happy to see his owner ignorant of all the craziness that his master had just been through. Nick knelt down in pain and let his buddy lick him all over the face. He inspected his stitches. The proud bulldog was in good shape. When Nick stood up Clarissa was there, Arnold's leash in her hand. He walked up to her and looked into her eyes cataloging her emotions.

"Beth and Frank were extremely close. Apparently, she had warned him not to go with you, but he told her that God had called his heart." Clarissa explained arms folded, eyeing Nick's blood-drenched thigh.

"Frank's the only reason any of us made it back. He was killed by a man that could've killed any of the best trained soldiers I ever fought with. He died honorably, Clarissa. He gave his life for everyone here without a single thought for his own safety. That level of commitment is what those who safeguard this camp must have. Maybe his death can mean that for your camp."

"You're not going to stay, are you?" Clarissa asked knowingly.

"I can't. But if Tommy gets his legs back he will be more than able to train up your members. He knows his way around a gun even better than I do."

"I'm sorry, Nick. You were right. We put people in harm's way without realizing what kind of trouble awaits us outside those gates. We need you to help us understand that."

"I'm sorry. I'll be leaving Arnold and Tommy here with you. I need you to do your best to keep them safe. All you need to know Frank's death is teaching you right now. Stay alert, remain vigilant, and don't ever let your guard down no matter how peaceful you think things seem."

"Okay." Clarissa hugged Nick and kissed him on his cheek. She gazed into his sharp grey eyes. "I just really don't understand you, Nick. Where could you possibly be going?"

"Believe me when I say that you don't want to know."

"Well, what about that?" Clarissa questioned pointing to Nick's thigh.

"Alcohol, some meds, and gauze are all I'll need. Stitches won't do any good. The wound is too shallow and spread too wide." Nick replied knowing a thing or two about battlefield medicine.

"Well, are you at least going to come to dinner tonight?" she asked not having a clue as to why Nick was being so mysterious. She knew it wasn't because he was being dramatic. She would get to the bottom of it before Nick left. Having him stay one more night was all the time she needed. She would press Melissa whom she had faith could garner Tommy's confidence. Melissa would find out everything she wanted to know for her. "A lot of hard work went into providing a tribute to not just you but Mark, Sarah, Roger, Lindo, and, of course, Frank. The camp could really use a couple of nice words from their heroes."

"I'll be asleep. Send somebody to wake me." Nick mumbled before turning on his heels. The tank of a bulldog bounded after his weary master happy as all get out to see him.

Clarissa turned and stood there for a while thinking. She had to handle this matter carefully. She would tell Melissa that she was afraid for Nick which wasn't far from the truth. But she needed something more, an added reason to convince Melissa to play on Tommy's heartstrings. The idea came to her in an instant. It was crude and sophomoric, but it would work. Assured of her strategy she went straight to Melissa's tent.

Q. J. Zephyr

Arnold bounded through the visitor tent's flap anxious to see Tommy whom he could smell inside. Arnold jumped onto Tommy's lap and the two shared a bunch of hugs and kisses. Nick couldn't help but notice that Tommy had been reading a book on theology. It was heavy reading for a newbie to the faith but knowing Tommy it was probably the first and only book he would ever need to read on the subject before understanding it completely, at least in principle.

"I see you're back in one piece. No worse for the wear. Haha," Tommy joked throwing a pillow at Nick who caught it and threw it back.

"Looks can be deceiving. I almost died today. One of the camp's members did die today." Nick sighed plopping down on his cot after pulling out a medkit from his bag of goodies. He took off his boots, pants, and vest and began applying an alcohol-drenched cotton ball to his wound. He clenched his teeth as the alcohol cleansed the gash in his thigh.

"Looks like you got bit by a gay leprechaun. Ouch." Tommy mused. "Is that the only chink in the chain?"

"Pretty much."

"Well, you did alright, then," Tommy added. "You still dead set on buying that one-way ticket to hell?"

"I'm gone in the morning."

"You are one crazy S.O.B., Nick." Tommy laughed shaking his head in amazement. "Here you are, a hero to the people of Maranatha, Clarissa to be had, and you're just gonna walk away from it all, for what? So you can do the death dance with a bunch of reptilians who have been waiting since they hatched out of giant eggs to rip you a new one."

"Yup. I'll trust you'll take good care of Arnold for me while I'm gone."

"What you mean to say is for the rest of his life. And you know I will even though he won't understand where you've gone." Bringing Tommy to his last argument for Nick staying, "It's just so selfish of you, man. Just stay. You know everyone is gonna find out sooner or later what the hell those things are. So, why rush it?"

"Because you don't know what you're talking about, Tommy. For all, we know everyone who went underground has flown to the moon. We don't even know if the shelters exist at all. Those people could have been walking straight into blast furnaces just like the Nazis had used. We won't ever know anything unless we risk ourselves trying to find out. Someone has got to get answers, Tommy. I can't sit here wondering about it all the time. Don't you understand?"

"You know I do." Tommy answered, "I just don't think you get where I'm coming from. That door that you want to open so badly is a metaphor for your life, Nick. It represents the abyss in your heart, in your mind, and your soul. You want answers that no one can provide for you. Even if you do find a whole mess of those things down there, you think they're just gonna be all, "Hey, Nick, this is our oldest oracle. Ask us anything and we'll grant you your magical wish"? Those things are gonna eviscerate you, tear you limb from limb like they did Jasper, and leave your self-righteous carcass, or whatever remains of it, to rot somewhere in their dark, stinky subterranean shit hole."

"Everything you're saying's true, Tommy. I can't argue with you. I never really could. You're good like that. Maybe you have found a reason to stay here beyond your newfound puppy love. But I'm going. That's all there is to it. Now if you don't mind I have to get some sleep. Like I said, I almost died today."

"Alright, Nick. While you're in the dream world see if you can seek out General Custer's dumbass. I'm sure he'll have some words of encouragement for ya."

Nick just laughed and closed his eyes. He fell asleep before Tommy could utter any more of his well-oiled remarks. Tommy just sat up with Arnold looking at his best friend, possibly for the last time. He had hoped to try and get some nookie from Melissa after dinner. They had already arranged a little date. And even though Tommy couldn't use his legs, he could use every other part of his body.

∞

Melissa's tent was on the southernmost edge of the camp. Being a physiotherapist, she had the right skills to become Clarissa's understudy. She wanted to be as close to the animal pens as needed so that she could provide them the best care possible. Melissa was a fast learner impressing Clarissa with her close to photographic memory at every turn. But Melissa wasn't ready for her camp's president to come into her tent and demand anything more from her than she was willing to give. She felt that Clarissa's request to speed up her blossoming affections for Tommy was not only unfounded but ungodly.

"I just can't believe you're asking me to do this," Melissa said.

"We have to find out where Nick is going, Melissa. There is something that man is hiding. Everything inside me tells me that whatever Nick and Tommy aren't telling us is crucial to this camp's wellbeing."

"Then just be honest and upfront with Nick. Go up to him and ask him yourself. Why do you need me to sleep with a paraplegic alcoholic to get the information you want?"

"I'm not asking you to sleep with him, Melissa, and don't you think I've tried? He won't tell me. I'm sorry but I just can't let this go. As the camp's leader, I have to put everyone else's lives ahead of my own. Now, someday I want you to run this camp. And you will have to be ready to make the same kinds of hard choices that I have to make every day."

"You make the hard choices? That's a joke, right, Clarissa?" Melissa argued her eyes watering. "Yes, you and the other camp leaders make the hard choices but who has to do all the hard work. Us! First, you send Mark and Sarah out into the wilderness for horse tranquilizers, and look what happened. Then you send Frank out to die to correct that mistake. And now you're asking me, knowing what I've been through, to give myself willingly to a man whose faith is questionable so that you can make some more hard choices. Give me a break, Clarissa."

"We have to know, Melissa." Clarissa pushed, "Just butter his biscuit enough to have him tell you what I need to know."

"I was raped, Clarissa! A year ago! One year. I came to this church seeking the help of Jesus Christ to see me through my hardship. And here I am at the foot of the cross and one of my church leaders is asking me to act against the will of my own heart. How could you?"

Clarissa knew that her suggestion might come to this. The fact was Melissa was so beautiful that she took great pains to make herself look unattractive. The messy hair, no make-up, and general disregard for her hygiene were just tools the young woman used to ward off potential mates, aggressors. But Clarissa had a will of her own and she wasn't about to take her foot off the gas pedal, not when something this important was on the line.

"You're not the only one that has suffered in that regard, Melissa. This isn't a pity party and this definitely isn't the way I would ever want to get this information. But the fact is we live in a world now where godless people do bad things to good people. There are no police anymore and there is no order beyond the walls of Maranatha. Frank's death has made that abundantly clear to everyone in this camp. Now to ensure the terrible things that happened to Mark, Sarah, and Frank won't happen again I need you to do this for me, for the camp. Now I tried to ask you politely thinking that you would put the camp's needs before your own problems. But I see now that this method is insufficient. So let me put it to you this way. You either do this for the camp or I will find another person to be my understudy. There are a lot of other qualified people who could replace you. Look, don't you understand? I don't want to have to threaten you like this. It was because of our shared trauma and our willingness to overcome it that I chose you to be my understudy because I knew you were strong and capable. But if you don't possess the temperament for leadership then I will find somebody with more guts." Clarissa finally got through. Melissa's countenance softened against Clarissa's wrought iron will. "C'mon, it'll be alright. Go wash your hair, put on some mascara, and put on something alluring, like a dress or something, okay?"

There was a long silent pause. Melissa had forgotten about the late nights at the church with the other battered women. She had forgotten about Clarissa's battle with a fire-breathing husband, supposedly a man of faith and a leader in her old Church. She respected Clarissa and there was no fight left in her. Melissa acquiesced to her leader's demands and summoned the courage to look into her mentor's impenetrable gaze without reproach.

"Okay." Melissa volunteered wiping tears from her plump, pale cheeks. Clarissa embraced her. "I should go get ready. I've got a lot of work to do. Tommy and I have a date tonight."

"Atta girl. Remember I'm not asking that you sleep with him or promise him anything. Just find out where Nick is going tomorrow, okay? It's a small thing, in the end, Melissa. I would never ask you to do anything I wasn't prepared to do myself. Never. Okay?"

"Okay."

"I'm proud of you. I'm sorry I had to say the things I did but I need this from you. Besides, Tommy's quite the looker, and if he tries anything just push his chair over." Clarissa laughed. Melissa managed to chuckle as she envisioned Tommy on their date wheeling himself around wherever they went.

She would find out what Clarissa wanted to know but not because she had threatened her. Melissa liked Tommy from the moment she first laid eyes on him. He was gregarious and honest, or so he seemed. To be that confident, without the use of his legs, spoke volumes about the man's character. Melissa showed Clarissa out and returned inside. The young woman slowly walked over to the darkest part of her tent where a full-length mirror that had once belonged to her grandmother stood. It was covered by an assortment of unfashionable clothes. Melissa threw them off piece by piece until her full reflection was revealed. She glanced hesitantly at herself and the person she had become. She let out a groan that came from deep inside her. Maybe it was time, she thought. Maybe this was God's way of telling her that it was okay to be beautiful again.

∞

The people of Maranatha gathered around Frank's wooden coffin holding photos of him and candles in their hands. It was a touching scene. But even though it was the Lance Corporal's funeral the real star of the show was wearing an emerald green dress and standing silently by Tommy's side. Nick couldn't believe how undeniably attractive Melissa was. Her flame-red hair had been brushed and straightened and lay over her shoulders like water spilling over a stone. Her tart green eyes were lit by the cool light of the moon above and the warm glow of the candles below. And her lips were so soft and pink that Nick imagined they tasted like strawberry taffy. She was certainly a sight to see. Every man in that camp did their best not to ogle the young lady during the ceremony. And Tommy was doing his best to hold back his toothy grin. He knew he was now the focus of great envy within the camp. The attention elevated Tommy's ego to a place even higher than it had been before he lost the use of his legs.

Nick refocused his thoughts on Frank and the garland of summer blooms that his wife had placed around the dead man's neck. Songs were sung, tears were shed, and people shared their testimonies about Frank's life. Nick had been asked to prepare a few kind words for the sake of Beth and the other campers. When it was his turn to speak Nick surprisingly became a little choked up.

"The only way you guys are going to survive out here is if every one of you becomes like Frank, who was willing to sacrifice himself to protect everyone in this camp. Take a look around you. This camp is your family. It's that simple. Lance Corporal Frank

Beverly was a proud member of the United States Marine Corps and a proud member of Maranatha. When I was asked to recover Mark and Sarah, Dennis had recommended him as the best shot in camp. But Frank wasn't just good. He performed his sharpshooting duties with skill equal to that of an Army Ranger or better. For someone who never went through sniper training that is saying a lot. He saved Roger's life for sure. The leader of the biker gang had a shotgun pointed dead at Roger and was about to use it when Frank, from over one hundred and fifty yards, away put a bullet straight through the man's brain. That's dedication, that's service, and that's how to protect the ones you value, the people you care for.

Before we left to go on our mission, just hours before Frank was to die, he asked me if I could do him a favor after thanking me for the opportunity to serve. I told him, 'sure, Frank, whatever you need.' He asked only that we pray for the mission. To be honest, his request touched me. The guy was

327

a little stiff and stern, but he was the 'real deal'. And he put every one of you ahead of himself without ever being asked to. He did it to protect you, his wife, and the camp. So, next time, when it's your turn to make a sacrifice, remember that you're no better than Frank and you're probably a whole helluva lot worse of a shot. I have never spoken at a fellow soldier's graveside before. But I just want to say thank you to a man who gave his life for something he believed in."

Nick stopped speaking and stepped back into the rank and file. People came up to Nick wanting nothing more than to thank him, to touch him, to pray for him. And as they lowered the dead marine into the earth Nick couldn't help but see himself in that grave. Why was his heart so set on seeking certain death? He had been welcomed into a group of fine people, the likes of which, probably couldn't be found for a thousand miles in any direction, and yet he was still compelled to leave it all behind. It was the creature, Nick surmised. All roads for him ended at the door in the mine.

The camp's leaders decided to have a late dinner after Frank's burial. It seemed the right thing to do. The sun had set and tepid breezes flowed through the camp playing with the loose fabric of people's clothes. Maranatha's band was playing soothing music behind the tables of the canteen. In the background images of Frank, Mark, and Sarah played on a large projection screen reminding everyone to be thankful as they feasted on BBQ chicken and roasted corn. Tommy and Melissa were glued at the hip and went off together to eat by themselves. He thought it strange that she got so dressed up for a funeral but chalked it up to there not being much to do for fun anymore. There were no clubs or vacation destinations or anything beyond survival, at least not yet. Nick got his food and sat down by himself like the last time he had eaten at the canteen. And just like the last time he was immediately swarmed by the camp's teenagers who wanted nothing more than to take pictures with him using their cell phones. He must have taken a thousand photos. He was so busy he didn't see Tommy and Melissa slip off into the night by themselves.

∞

Tommy held Melissa's right hand as he pushed the wheels of his chair forward with his left. They strolled and rolled out to the horse paddocks. It was one of the quieter places in the camp and was Melissa's favorite spot to spend time alone with her thoughts. They stopped to feed a healthy brown mare some carrots. Tommy, not knowing how to properly feed a horse, almost got his fingers crushed by the mare's blunt teeth. Thankfully, Melissa pulled Tommy's forearm back just in time. They shared a pleasant laugh before Tommy decided to heat things up.

"You know I really like you, don't ya?" Tommy admitted having no other choice but to look up to Melissa. Sensing a moment brewing she sat on his lap giving up some, but not all, of her height advantage.

"I like you, too, Tommy."

"Y'know, you didn't have to get all dolled up for me. I like ya just the way you are when you roll out of bed and go messin' around with them horses."

"It wasn't for you." Melissa cracked up hitting Tommy on his shoulder, "It was for Frank. I wanted to dress up for Frank's funeral."

"Lemme get this straight. You dressed up prettier than a brand new Cadillac for a dead man when you got a live, passion pumping man right here? Naw, I don't buy that one bit, darlin'."

Melissa just laughed. Tommy was funny, exciting and his current disability made it much easier to handle him. She leaned in and kissed him long and strong. She had planned to pull back but she became unforeseeably drunk with Tommy's affections. They made out for hours by the horses and the cottonwoods. Finally, after minutes of losing themselves in each other's eyes, Melissa asked the question Clarissa wanted to know the answer to. She pulled away from Tommy and gave him a look that betrayed her thoughts.

"Well, don't just sit there looking pretty. Tell me what's on your mind?"

"It's about Nick. Y'know, word around camp is that he's leaving tomorrow. Nobody wants to see him go. Tommy, where could he possibly be going that he would leave behind his best friend and his bulldog? It just doesn't make any sense."

"I know. I tried telling him to stay put but he wouldn't listen. I'm afraid, in that regard, there's not much I can do. Now, as, to where he's going, well, I just can't tell you that. You would have to get Nick to tell you. He would be madder than hell if I said anything about it."

"Oh, yeah, well, you know what they say, a pretty girl likes a challenge, especially when it comes to secrets." Melissa teased unbuttoning Tommy's shirt and kissing his chest. She couldn't believe her forwardness, but she was enjoying herself for the first time in a long time. "Tell me, Tommy, and I'll take you back to my tent."

Tommy sat back in his wheelchair and cocked his head to the side in disbelief. Had he read her wrong when they first met, he thought? He wasn't sure if she was acting out of character or was truly smitten by him. Maybe it was both. In any case, he hadn't been with a woman in a while. And Melissa was so beautiful he had no choice but to give in. Besides, he thought, if the people wanted to know about the lizards then, hell, let 'em know about the dang lizards. There was no sense in keeping it from them if they wanted to know. He figured Nick would be dead in a day or two and then it wouldn't even matter. He nodded his head signing onto the deal.

"Is a bit of gossip worth that much around here?" Tommy asked.

"Let's just say inquiring minds want to know." Melissa wiggled her hips adjusting her position on Tommy's lap just right. She kissed him again and in a voice cut from a length of silk asked, "Tommy, tell me where Nick is going?"

"I'll do better than that lil' darlin'. I'll show ya."

∞

Nick was sharing a cigar with Kai and Dennis. They were stretched out around one of the picnic tables in front of the canteen. The rest of the campers had cleared out hours ago and the three of them were sipping on a thirty year-old bottle of Scotch that Dennis had been saving for a special occasion. They were having a great conversation about a wide range of topics. Nick felt at home with the older fellas and even though he came to like them very much he was no closer to staying than he had ever been. It was late and it was time for Nick to say his goodbyes. Kai and Dennis embraced Nick and wouldn't let him leave without praying over him. When they were done Nick thanked them humbly. Buzzing like a firefly he stumbled off toward his tent. But before he even made it halfway there he came upon Clarissa standing in the middle of his path waiting for him. She seemed particularly perturbed about something. Nick paid her no mind. He wasn't married to the woman nor were they bumpin' uglies. He didn't owe her a damn thing under the blue sky. Nick was content to walk right around her when she stepped directly into his path.

"You were never going to tell us were you?" Clarissa's words seemed to poke out of her mouth and into Nick's chest. "You were just going to let us remain in ignorance knowing full well the danger we might be in."

"What are you talking about?" Nick asked caught off guard. He didn't even want to know the answer to his question. He just wanted to go to sleep.

"This. This is what I'm talking about!" Clarissa whipped out her cell phone and held it up to Nick's face. He was confronted with a photo of the preserved reptilian's head from the cooler in the back of his truck.

"Where'd you get that?" Nick asked in disbelief knowing full well Tommy was the culprit.

"I rummaged through your stuff, Nick." Clarissa lied wanting to cover her tracks. "I wanted to know where you were going. I bet it's got something to do with this. What is it, Nick, and why would you bring that thing here?"

"I don't what it is, Clarissa. It's definitely not a bear." Nick laughed. The Scotch gave Nick a bit more edge to his personality than was normal. "Now you see why I can't stay. Look, three days ago we had the fight of our lives against that thing. It came out of an old mine up near Lake Arrowhead.

I'm going back into that mine tomorrow to search for answers. I have no idea what I'll find or even if I'll make it out alive."

Clarissa satisfied with Nick's response thought for a moment before speaking, "I don't want to see you go, Nick. You know that. The whole camp wants you to stay. You make them feel safe. But this changes things and, please, when you do go tomorrow morning make sure you take whatever that thing is as far away from this camp as possible. You were right not to tell me about it. Good luck, Nick. Good night, and goodbye." Clarissa wasn't sentimental at all with her farewell and it was for the best. Nick had to get some sleep. He was off in the morning to play a hand of cards with Death who he knew was waiting for him.

Tommy had spent the night in Melissa's tent leaving Nick and Arnold alone to spend one last night together. He slept soundly and when the cock's crow woke him the next day he began packing all of his stuff in his big sea bag. He stockpiled everything he would need to not only open the searing hot hatch but also storm into it killing whatever needed to die. He fed Arnold and kissed him one last time before heading to the canteen for breakfast. Nick ate like it was his last meal. He had waffles with butter and syrup, hash browns, two eggs, and three pieces of bacon. He washed it all down with two cups of fresh-squeezed orange juice. After saying goodbye to the kitchen staff and some of the other campers Nick walked out to his truck parked at the edge of the dirt lot. Melissa and Tommy were waiting beside it holding hands. They both had the look. There was something about the way they were standing there that made Nick feel as though he would never see the two of them again. It was as if his mind had taken a snapshot of them for the sake of his memory in advance of their absence in his life.

"Well, bud, this is where our roads diverge in the great wood," Tommy said holding out his arm.

"I wish you the best, Nick. I really do. You're the finest 'blackjack' I ever did meet."

"Thank you, Tommy. But I'll see you guys again soon." Nick lied. "Take care of Arnold for me until I get back. It was nice meeting, you Melissa. You've got your work cut out for you, but I'd trust him with my own life."

"Thank you, Nick, for everything. Please be safe. Don't forget to pray!" Melissa offered.

That was all Nick needed to hear before jumping into his pickup and heading down the long road to the camp's front entrance. He took his time leaving and when he finally made it to the gates Kai was standing there waiting for him.

"Here, a little parting gift from the boys in the band." Kai handed Nick three hand-rolled cigarillos that stunk with the pungent smell of marijuana. He also passed a thermos through the window that was filled with something hot. "Cowboy coffee. Made it over the fire this morning just for you, bud. It's been a real pleasure, Nick. I'm sad to see ya go. Maybe when you come back you'll have a darn good story to tell. Whaddya say?"

"Absolutely. You're wearing the biggest pair in camp, Kai. Make sure Dennis gets your guys trained up. You never know what might be lurking out there. Take care." Nick said shaking Kai's long slender hand before pulling away from the gate. He sparked up one of Kai's cigarillos. It was a nice smoke. He looked back into his rearview at Kai and the gates of Maranatha wondering if he would ever be able to know peace, to be at rest. By the end of the day, it probably wouldn't even matter. Nick pushed on the gas, turned a country corner, and was gone.

The 9 Orders: The Collection

Q. J. Zephyr

About

The Author

Q. *J. Zephyr* was born in San Diego, California in 1979. Zephyr went on to graduate from the Art Center's Graduate School of the Arts where he graduated in 2011 with a degree in fine arts. He became an art history and studio arts teacher and traveled the world bringing the joy of visual learning wherever he went.

It was during this sojourn, which began in 2013, that Zephyr began writing his epic high stakes adventure The Nine Orders. It has always been Zephyr's goal to not only entertain his readers but to leave them with a sense of profound insight into the origins of human civilization.

343

Q. J. Zephyr